Stealing Wishes

Books by Shannon Yarbrough

THE OTHER SIDE OF WHAT

STEALING WISHES

Stealing Wishes

Shannon Yarbrough

TOSOW PUBLISHING
SAINT LOUIS

STEALING WISHES

© 2008 by Shannon Yarbrough
www.shannonyarbrough.com

ToSow Publishing

ISBN: 978-0-6152-1361-3

Printed in the United States of America

10 9 8 7 6 5 4 3 2 1

For John

It's been a long time since that first cup, but I still look forward to coffee with you every morning.

I had some dreams, they were clouds in my coffee.

~Carly Simon,
You're So Vain

If I could make a wish, I think I'd pass.
Can't think of anything I need.

~The Everly Brothers,
The Air That I Breathe

One

This is something you may or may not know.

In 1939, Christopher Isherwood wrote a book called *Goodbye to Berlin* in which he said, "I am a camera with its shutter open, quite passive, recording, not thinking." His novel was made into a play and later a film in 1955 under the name *I Am a Camera.* The play inspired a stage musical called *Cabaret* in 1966, which inspired a film in 1972 of the same name.

Isherwood died in 1986, so he lived to see all of this take place. True life inspired his words, which inspired a film, which inspired a play (more words), which inspired another film. And now, it inspires my words. This is my true life.

Isherwood was right when he wrote those words. I too am a camera. Where are the candid shots of me? No one has ever taken them. Turning the pages of my photo album one might ask, "Where are all the pictures of you, Blaine?"

There aren't any. I am the one behind the camera. The photographer—No! The camera! Yes, I was at that pool party, that birthday party, that July 4th picnic. I snapped that picture of you with the bunny ears. I snapped you making that big splash, and the one with your trunks down. I told everyone to smile cheesy for the camera, to look my way on the count of three.

"You have such a good eye. You should do this for a living," I'm told.

But I don't. Cameras are just a leisure pursuit.

We all have something we are good at that we'd rather be doing, but instead we flip burgers, or wait tables and pour coffee. We put on a suit and go to an office, or we drive heavy machinery. We all want to be firemen or teachers or doctors when we grow up. No kid tells the class they want to be a telemarketer or a housecleaner. A harsh reality shatters our dreams and just maybe a twist of fate puts us where we want to be, instead of in front of the stove or behind the desk. Some of us still dream.

We wouldn't call it work if we got paid to do what we

really wanted to do, would we? I'd love to get paid to be a photographer, but then I probably wouldn't enjoy taking pictures as much. And so I am a camera, but draw a paycheck for working behind the counter in a coffee shop. When I'm not pouring coffee, I take pictures.

Do you know those events in life when something extraordinary happens like a home run, a first step, the perfect catch, or a pretty snowfall? It's one of those moments that you want to remember forever. It deserves a page in the scrapbook. It's a story you'd have to show to everyone at the office to get them to believe it. What do you always say just as it happens?

"I wish I had a camera right now!"

In my life, I always have the camera. I am always equipped to capture those vital and momentous threads of life that our mind can't and won't hold onto. I'm prepared, but the trouble is my life is often lacking those threads that hold it together. I can count on one hand the number of times I've experienced something meaningful that was worth capturing on film. And even then, I probably left the lens cap on.

Instead, I take pictures of other's memories-to-be, mostly when they aren't looking. Everywhere I go, I am surrounded by them, but people are too wrapped up in their lives to be paying attention. In the park there's an old man daydreaming on a park bench, a little girl in a pink dress feeding pigeons, or a black alley cat in a bush stalking a squirrel. These are my memories, the ones that matter to me now. No birthday cake candles. No winning touch downs. No beach vacations. Just life, raw and not overexposed.

At some point in this life, I will have to face the digital eye myself. But when? Will I be a John Doe on a cold chrome laboratory table all puffy and bruised beneath the slow flash? Is this my close up? Am I ready? At the parlor, my casket might as well be closed because when I'm six feet under there won't be any Polaroids to thumb through to remind you what I looked like.

You probably think you now know all you need to know.

Not yet.

Two

The alarm clock is on the dresser across the room and it is set for 5:32am. If it was on the nightstand, I'd hit the snooze button and risk getting up at an odd time which would ruin my entire day. If the day doesn't start correctly, it's not worth getting out of bed for.

That's only happened once since I started working at the coffee shop eight years ago. There was a power outage in the middle of the night that reset my alarm clock to twelve o'clock twelve o'clock twelve o'clock, so it wasn't my fault I was late. My boss told me not to worry about it, but I beat myself up for weeks after that and have never been late since.

I do tend to wake up in the middle of the night, only to get out of bed and check to make sure the alarm clock is still set for the correct time. I know it is because I check it at least twice before getting into bed, but my mind assumes some imaginary ghost might creep into the room while I'm sleeping and change the alarm.

Or maybe it's that I'm afraid I was a bit too sleepy and my mind deceived me when I was getting ready for bed. Maybe I set the alarm for 5:23am instead of 5:32am, although that's never happened before. It shouldn't matter if I got up early, but that's nine minutes early. I'd have to stay in bed at least one more minute, not daring to get up an odd number of minutes before I was supposed to. But, if I waited a minute then it might actually be 5:33am and I'd be late already. I'd have to call into work sick.

I'm usually awake five to ten minutes before the alarm goes off. That happens to most people, I'm sure. It's your body's way of preparing itself for what's to come. Your mind is always early, but if by chance I forgot to set the alarm clock then my mind would probably not wake up at all. My mind knows the alarm isn't going to go off, so there's no reason to wake the body to let you know the alarm isn't set. Your mind already knows the alarm isn't set, because it forgot to remind you to set it before you went to bed. Your mind likes to play tricks on your body.

It's sort of like when skinny girls order a latte at the coffee shop and refrain from putting sugar in it because they think they look fat.

So, I check the alarm twice before bed and once in the middle of the night, and although I sometimes wake up a few minutes early I keep my eyes shut and I do not look at the clock until the alarm actually goes off. I know on some days I wake up two minutes before the alarm sounds, and on other days I wake up as much as seven minutes early. Not being able to control those few minutes of drifting out of my sleep because my body is ready to get up would drive me crazy, so I just pretend it doesn't happen. Although I am usually already awake, when the alarm sounds at 5:32am I open my eyes and get out of bed to shut it off just as I should. There's no reason to let the alarm think it's doing a bad job.

My alarm is a long sustained *beep* that repeats over and over again. *Beep... beep... beep.* I never understood those people who have a clock radio and use it as an alarm, waking up to music playing or to the voices of their favorite morning radio show. I couldn't grasp waking up to something different everyday. My mind would probably wake the body hours before the alarm, just in anticipation of what was going to play when the alarm goes off. What would the alarm surprise us with this morning? Who's to say I'd even wake up? What if at 5:32am the radio program was observing a long moment of silence? My alarm would actually be going off, but I'd hear nothing but silence. Can you even hear silence? What if that moment of silence lasted longer than a minute and the music didn't resume until 5:35am?

You guessed it. I'd be two minutes late and have to call in sick.

Today, as always, I'm on time. I immediately set the alarm clock again for 5:48am allowing myself sixteen minutes to use the bathroom, shave, and shower. Sixteen is half of thirty-two, so if there is something that I know I'm going to probably do twice a day I prefer to take sixteen minutes to do it each time. Since I'm awake, I practically have my morning routine down to an art form without having to check the clock twice.

I usually finish in the bathroom before the alarm sounds letting me know my sixteen minutes are up. If I do take the full sixteen minutes then the alarm sounds at 5:48am. That leaves me fourteen minutes to get dressed before 6:02am. I prefer to be out of bed and ready for work by that time. If I spend a few minutes less in the shower on any given morning, I can sometimes beat the bathroom alarm by two minutes. This gives me sixteen minutes to get dressed instead.

I don't mentally prepare myself for this sixteen minute interval to take place everyday. Remember, I use the sixteen minute time frame only if there's something I know I'm going to do twice a day so that the total time doing it adds up to thirty-two. Getting dressed in the morning also entails brushing my teeth and combing my hair so twelve to sixteen minutes is plenty of time, but undressing in the evening and brushing my teeth before bed only takes about four minutes.

Taking off my clothes is the opposite of what I do in the morning and takes no time at all, and I rarely comb my hair in the evening. So, the only act I'm doing twice a day here is brushing my teeth which I do for a minimum of three minutes both in the morning and at night anyway. Splitting thirty-two minutes between these two routines just doesn't seem feasible to me. I guess I could set the alarm and take longer to get undressed at night, but that seems a bit absurd. I've heard of people changing clothes several times in the morning, trying to get their outfit just right. I've done it myself before when I was too many minutes ahead of schedule. But how many times do we undress in the evening? There is no wrong way to take our clothes off, is there? So if I'm too far ahead of schedule in the day it's much easier to make up for it in the morning by taking a minute or two longer to ready myself for the work day ahead.

At 6:02am, I go into the kitchen to make breakfast. I eat hot oatmeal with a banana for breakfast three times a week and cereal with cold milk on the other two days. I'm not counting weekends here. I alternate these each week, having oatmeal twice and cereal three times on the second and fourth weeks of the month. I go through thirty-two bananas a month, sometimes using one whole banana and half of another if I'm only having oatmeal twice that week. I go through five boxes of oatmeal because three plus two equals five. I'll tell you more about *five* later. And for cereal, I make it a habit of buying three boxes and two gallons of milk each month.

I don't want to spend too much time telling you my thoughts on the calendar and the way if affects my schedule. Let's just say I wish each month had thirty-two days, instead of most of them only having thirty-one. It would make things much easier. April, June, September, and November are even worse. We won't mention February.

Three

While eating breakfast, I sit on the sofa and watch the morning news on Channels 2 or 3. I'd much prefer to watch Channel 32 but it's just cartoons all day long. Okay, so I watch it sometimes. I leave my apartment at 6:32am to walk to work. Did I mention that my apartment number is also thirty-two? How cool is that? I live on the second tier (of three), and there are thirty-two steps to get to the ground landing. My apartment building is on Roosevelt Avenue, and yes, Roosevelt was the 32nd president of the United States.

You are probably thinking, "Blaine, there's no way your entire life can revolve around the number 32, right?"

That is correct. But, if you add three and two together it equals five, remember? I prefer not to get involved in intervals or derivatives of five. Five is an odd number, so I only use it when my daily life does not mold itself to my much preferred number of 32. Five is my safe number. For instance, the coffee shop where I work is five blocks from my apartment, but I can walk there in a total of 160 steps. 160 divided by 5 equals 32.

Did I forget to mention that I am 32 years old?

The coffee shop is called The Latte Da. I am one of only three employees there including the owner, Sallie. Even though I don't have to be at work until 7am when the shop opens, I usually arrive a bit early because it doesn't take 28 minutes to walk five blocks. When we open right at 7am, there's usually an early morning rush so it's nice to have a few minutes to prepare for them. Although she has never said anything, I know that Sallie appreciates my promptness.

Being a coffee barista is challenging. Pushing the last legal drug, caffeine, can be quite an art form and customers take their sippable art quite seriously. I can't remember the last time I poured a plain black coffee. There's Hazelnut, Southern pecan, Cinnamon, Aztec cocoa, Hawaiian blend, Mexican blend, Breakfast blend, Sumatra, and about a dozen other flavored coffees on our menu. I don't think the word "plain" exists in coffee vocabulary. Then there are the flavored syrups customers can add to their drink for (you guessed it!) thirty-two cents extra, of which The Latte Da has thirty-two flavors. So, your Hazelnut coffee becomes Cherry Hazelnut. Your Breakfast blend becomes Caramel Breakfast blend. Your Cinnamon coffee becomes Cinnamon Apple.

And that's just coffee.

I haven't mentioned the mochas, lattes, cappuccinos, and macchiatos. When you add a shot of espresso to milk or water, a chemical reaction takes place creating a new Italian-sounding name that is somehow responsible for dividing customers into social classes. If you step up to the counter and order a "half-caf grande soy mocha with a shot of caramel, shot of almond, extra shot of chocolate, with little foam and hold the whip cream," people respect you.

For those who are not so rehearsed in the argot of ordering, there's the simple latte. It's nothing more than a shot of espresso in steamed milk, but just uttering the word "latte" has been known to build confidence. Newcomers have stood to the side for up to ten minutes perusing the menu like it was a flight schedule in a Chinese airport, only to step up to the counter and order a small latte. They breathe easy knowing the nerve-wrecking task is done. It's up to Blaine, the barista, to finish from there. I savor the look on their face when they take that first sip and expect to taste some sugary, chocolate, ice cream kiddy goodness. Their eyes twitch, their lips pucker, their head shakes, and I just point them in the direction of the condiment counter where they will poison their purchase with six packets of Sweet n Low.

"You should have made a suggestion," Sallie used to tell me.

"They didn't ask."

The truth is I don't want to be the one responsible for them not liking what they order. If they at least picked it out themselves, they are at fault and probably won't feel so bad about spending a lot of money on a latte. Who is to say they are going to like what I suggest? The first time I ever tried sushi I hated it.

That was probably because I tried what the waiter suggested, which was also the most expensive thing on the menu. It ended up costing him part of his tip, but I at least went back and tried it again. I just ordered something different and found a dish I liked. It works the same with coffee. How else are they going to learn?

Sallie always likes to ask every customer if they want to add a flavor shot to their drink because it increases sales. She calls it up-selling. If one hundred people add a flavor shot, it adds 32 dollars to our sales for the day. I concentrate more on asking people to purchase a bagel or doughnut. Bagels and doughnuts are one to two dollars each. If one hundred people purchase a pastry, that's anywhere from one to two hundred dollars added to our daily sales.

"Every dollar counts," Sallie chimes.

That's true, but customers are picky about their coffee. We see the same faces in here everyday and they order the same thing. I don't even have to ask half of them what they want. If it's a quick fix, I can practically have it ready by the time they reach the cash register because I know who they are and I know what they drink. When it comes to coffee, the majority of people don't like change. It's pretty much that way with anything that soothes our thirst or hunger.

It's also part of our daily routine in life. Customers like coming in everyday on their way to work and getting their Caramel Macchiatos or Almond Joy Mochas. They like getting to see Sallie or myself because they like the way we make their drink. They trust us. It practically guarantees repeat business when the customer is satisfied. If some business lady has come in everyday for the past two years and ordered a non-fat cocoa every single day, why would I suggest a shot of banana syrup if she turned down the up-sell the day before?

"She might change her mind today," Sallie has said.

And what if she does change her mind? What if she tells us to go ahead with that shot of amaretto or banana today? What if she gets in her car and sits the drink down in the cup holder to answer her cell phone? She drives off and gets on the freeway to go to work. She finishes with her phone call and reaches down for her non-fat banana amaretto flavored cocoa and takes a sip.

She hates it and spits it out all over the windshield, and now she can't see. She's doing sixty on the freeway and reaches for a napkin to try to wipe the windshield, but she spills the rest of the hot cocoa in her lap. She's wearing a black mini skirt that day to impress her boss so the cocoa burns her legs.

Without thinking, she pushes down on the gas pedal because she's shaking her legs wildly from the sting of the hot drink. She swerves in traffic because she still can't see out the cocoa covered windshield. The car changes lanes wildly and hits a couple of other cars. She crashes into the concrete median and six other cars pile up. Four people are killed instantly, including the business lady. Was her 32 cents worth it? What does Sallie think about all of this?

"I'm glad we have hot beverage warnings on our lids."

Four

You should probably know that Sallie claims to be bisexual. Not only is she my employer, but she is also my best friend. I do not know if Sallie has ever slept with a woman, nor do I want to know. Sallie and I tried to have sex once several years ago, but it didn't work. I don't mean "it" as in my penis; I just mean the act of having sex with one another never happened.

It was "couples night out." We call it that because neither one of us ever go on dates, but we still want to go out and have fun. So, we just go together and do whatever dating couples would normally do. We go out to eat, we go to bars, we go dancing, or we go to movies. It just depends on our mood.

On this particular night, we had dinner at a college bar. We both like pub food and beer, so we've hit almost every joint in town by now. There have been very few bars that we've visited twice. I could probably count those on one hand. After each of us had about a pitcher of beer, it was still early and we decided to go dancing. I took her to a gay bar called Backstreet, which is within walking distance of my apartment, where the walls vibrate to techno and 80s pop remixes all hours of the night.

Our beer buzz aided in the naughty dancing beneath the disco ball and bright blinking lights. Most gay people look better in the dark, and why do they always rub on one another on the dance floor? Is it a lack of rhythm or a desire to be the first fully clothed porn star? I bump into more protruding penises and boobs that way it seems, and no one cares. I zig zag my way off the dance floor like a kid going through a turnstile to get on a ride at the county fair; I say excuse me whenever I bump into a tit or a tent. I turn back to acknowledge them to their face and mouth an apology. The girls flicker their eyes at me like they think I am hitting on them. The guys flash a coy grin and flicker their eyes too when all I want to do is get through the humps and bumps to take a piss.

Sallie follows because she needs to pee too. The

bathrooms are co-ed, after all we are in a gay men's bar that doesn't cater willingly to straight women. There are no doors on the stall so she needs me to stand guard while she squats. I hold her purse with my back turned to her. Other guys and girls come and go past me, but I'm not embarrassed standing there with her faux croc purse in my hand. Club goers with fag hags know this routine all too well. I hear the toilet flush behind me as she finishes. She stands at the mirror and reapplies lipstick and mascara while I take my turn at the urinal.

"Need me to hold anything?" Sallie jokes.

I ignore her.

After the bathroom break, we head to the bar and each do two shots of tequila before ordering drinks. Sallie prefers to drink wine or martinis, anything that comes in a glass with a stem. I prefer what Sallie calls a girly drink, anything with fruit or an umbrella. Besides beer, give me a beverage that is orange, red, pink, or teal with a kabob of pineapple and cherries and I'm a happy man. We sit and people-watch through two rounds of cocktails and then get back on the dance floor to bump and grind with strangers.

Dancing seems to be a much safer form of sex these days, and the answer to a voyeur's prayers. You can do it with as many people as you want all in one night, or stand against the wall and watch. The consequences are minimal, but if you participate your rhythm may tarnish your reputation nonetheless. Sallie and I circle around her heels and purse in the corner, like African tribe members worshipping the spirits of the animals sacrificed for her apparel. Two shirtless young men approach us, invading our tribal circle but we let them because they are gorgeous. They gyrate and trade sweat between us. One of them reaches for Sallie and pulls her between them to simulate a *ménage trios* dance move.

Feeling left out, I position myself behind the guy in the back. I rest my hands on his waist and swish my hips back and forth to his beat. He reaches for my arms and wraps them around his slick washboard waist. The front of my shirt is now clinging to his cool wet back. The salty smell of his hair and of his Calvin

Klein cologne invades my nostrils. The room spins. If I had my camera, I would have taken our picture because this is definitely a moment no one else would believe in the morning.

What happened next is fuzzy in my brain. Remember, the mind plays tricks on you. Maybe I just dreamt this, but I want to say that the four of us ended up on the bar's patio to share a joint and a heavy make-out session. On other days, I remember us taking the boys back to my apartment for a hot forgy. But in reality neither of those things happened.

Our two hunky jocks were lovers and they wandered off when the song was over. We watched them couple off to grope each other and tongue wrestle. One can only imagine the pornographic romance they created in their bedroom that night! Sallie and I went to the patio to inhale the second hand smoke of other joint smokers. Neither of us likes weed enough to purchase it for ourselves. Some time after 3am we walked back to my apartment. I made us pancakes.

Still drunk and high, we sat on the sofa and at some point heavy kissing followed. Attempting to pick up where the dance floor left off, we fumbled toward the bedroom leaving behind a trail of bar-soaked stinky clothes. Naked, I climbed on top of her like a kid racing up a hill. Not knowing what to put where, I assumed everything would fall into its proper place. But by then Sallie had passed out beneath me. I leaned back to look at her snoring face. Reality slapped me across the face and I turned over and quickly passed out myself. This was a night Sallie would never remember. And one I would never mention, and so my mind changed it.

Five

You could say a camera also tricks the mind. Over or under exposure of film can cause smoky images that look like cemetery fog, or maybe a finger or camera strap got in the way of your perfect shot. Even the flash reflected off of microscopic particles of dust makes us think we see orbs or alien ghost lights floating on walls or around people. When the photo develops, we see what we want to see, what we want to believe. A smart photographer could make these spoofs seem intentional, bending the light and using simple techniques to capture the essence of his subject in motion; all with the correct use of the flash and the shutter.

A fast shutter speed will freeze your subject and a slow shutter speed will make it look blurred as the subject moves. You can also combine flash with a slow speed to get movement and blur all in the same shot. Suddenly, your ghosts have become photogenic, but still unseen to the naked eye. The camera lens can see them. But no one is perfect. My hair still gets in the way and ruins the shot I was hoping for, or I suffer from a slow finger and the bird flies away.

Any novice might throw those mottled photos in the trash, wanting only the unsullied snapshots worthy enough for the family photo album. I keep every photo I take, the ideal images and not so ideal. Cameras don't trick the mind. If anything, they help the mind remember. But who wants to remember the mistakes they made, unintentional or not?

Six

In a 1973 interview, Christopher Isherwood said, "It seems to me that the real clue to your sex orientation lies in your romantic feelings rather than in your sexual feelings. If you are really gay, you are able to fall in love with a man, not just enjoy having sex with him."

I covet my friendship with Sallie. She is the only person in this city who I don't get tired of seeing everyday of my life. She understands me, and she likes to think that I understand her. She says I do, but I'm still not sure. Of course, I love her like any friend should love another. I could spend the rest of my life with her, and not get bored. It'd just be easier, I think. But Sallie needs a man who can love her both romantically and sexually, and I just don't think I can do that. She wishes she could change me, my sexuality. She's even said so.

"I wish you could just be straight," she's said a thousand times before.

"I wish you could just be a man," I always replied.

"If I knew you'd never leave me, I'd wish for it on my next birthday."

"You'd wish for me to never leave you or you'd wish to be a man?" I ask.

"Both."

Neither of us has slept with a man in months, much less felt romantic towards one. Maybe that's why Sallie considers herself to be bisexual. If the right man (or woman) comes along, she'll take what she can get. Being bisexual or homosexual really comes down to the actual sex part. That's why sex is part of the word.

I've never had sex with a woman, nor have I ever wanted to. I think the liquor and the dance floor were to blame for what almost happened between Sallie and me that night. But then again, nothing happened. I prefer to have sex with men. Well, I guess I shouldn't say "prefer". Preference makes you sound like you have a choice in the matter, so I should say I want to have sex with men. I like sex with men.

It's the relationship part, the part outside of sex, that I just can't see myself being good at. I never wanted to come home to someone, kiss them good-night, and lie down in bed next to them for a lifetime. And then there's my obsessive compulsiveness. How would I fit someone else into my routine? Date 32 men all at once, perhaps?

Relationships and romance are easy to ignore. You can just choose to be alone in life, I guess. It's the sex part that's a little trickier. Our bodies all have desires, and sooner or later it's nice to have someone else in the room to satisfy them. If sex wasn't the issue, I think I'd choose Sallie.

Seven

Once I've walked down the 32 steps outside the apartment, I take 32 steps to get one block down Roosevelt to Madison Avenue. From there, I turn west and take 128 steps down Madison four more blocks to get to The Latte Da. Sallie is already inside stocking the pastry case. She usually arrives at work at 6am to bake fresh pastries and to start making coffee. I have a key so I let myself in. She looks up when she hears the bell on the door chime announcing my arrival.

"Good morning, Sunshine," she says with a big toothy grin.

Sallie has a very bubbly personality, so I think nothing of her cheery mood.

"What's so good about it?" I grumble.

"Well, you aren't going to believe it but I have a date tonight!"

I knew eventually one of us would mutter those words. Neither of us is good at keeping secrets, and we tell each other everything. So, there was no reason for her not to tell me her good news. I always knew she'd be the one to find a date first. It's easier for women, I think, although that doesn't explain why neither of us has had a date in over two years. But that's in the past now. This very moment changes everything. Sallie has a date. I haven't decided yet how happy I am for her, or how jealous. I pretend to be interested.

"What's their name?"

Notice I said *their* instead of *he* or *she*?

"*His* name is Charlie."

"So, it's to be a man between us," I reply.

I draw us each a shot of espresso. Our typical routine right before opening is to do a shot, but based on today Sallie will probably tell me next she prefers cold milk. I hand her the shot glass. We toast and empty the glasses. The hot bitter liquid stings my taste buds almost as much as Sallie's announcement. I remain quiet as I prep the espresso machine during those last moments before the café opens. Sallie has finished with the pastry case and counts the cash register. There are two or three people already waiting outside the door.

I expect Sallie to offer up more information about Charlie. She knows the sudden news of her date has shaken me, so she is quiet. I know that men will come and go in both of our lives, but our friendship will still be the thread that brings us back together. Rather than forcing her to keep the words bottled up that she so badly wants to spit out, I speak up.

"How did you meet Charlie?"

"I arrived at work this morning and was fumbling with the front door a few minutes like always. I hate that damn lock. I dropped my keys and knelt to pick them up. When I stood back up he was just standing there. He startled me because it was like he just appeared out of nowhere…"

He appeared out of nowhere. The first encounter is always magical. She could have met him last night at home on a sex hotline and just be making this entire story up, but the first encounter always has to be magical. I think I would believe her more if she told me the sex hotline bit. Do women even call hotlines for phone sex?

"…He asked me what time we open. I told him. Then, he introduced himself and said he was new in town."

A newcomer. That was bad because there was no way to find out his deepest darkest secrets from anyone else who might have dated him, or someone who might be related. We'd have to find out everything on our own. I say "we" because if Sallie continues to date this guy steadily, she'll learn only what she needs to know as they get to know each other. It'll be the sugar-coated goodness that his Mommy taught him. He'll open the car door and doors to restaurants for her. He'll clean his apartment and take out the trash, hide the dirty clothes under the bed. He'll buy her a toothbrush for when she sleeps over; he'll scrub his toilet, and probably send her flowers for no reason. She'll fall for him. Girls always do.

I'll learn the other stuff that Sallie looks over. Blinded by love, her glassy eyes won't see past the fluff. They'll be married with a bun in the oven before she learns he dropped out of college, or has two DUI's, maybe he even spent time in prison. She won't know that he doesn't floss or clean the toilet. He leaves dirty clothes on the kitchen table, or only vacuums when company comes over. By then, it might be too late for Sallie. But I'll know. I'll make it my personal vendetta to learn all that I can about this Charlie guy and warn Sallie before she says "I do." Hell, I'll even take pictures!

"He's coming in later to take me to lunch, so you'll get to meet him," Sallie finishes.

I drop a shot glass. It shatters on the tile floor.

"What?" I ask.

"I'm going to lunch with him today."

"Is this the date?"

"I guess you could call it that. I'm calling it that. So, yeah. Yeah. It's *the* date."

"No pick me up at seven? No choosing shoes and dresses, or how to fix your hair? No make-up tips? No movie? No restaurant—"

"Blaine!" She interrupted my rant, "I haven't been on a date like that since high school!"

"Sallie, it's 6:45 in the morning and you have frosting on your blouse. There's flour in your hair."

"Maybe Charlie likes frosting."

Eight

Maybe he likes frosting, she says? Maybe he likes kitchen knives and handcuffs. I couldn't fathom going on a date with someone without first asking for a resume, reference check, and a urine sample. Sure, I'd be willing to sleep with them without the urine sample first, but a date is a commitment.

"It's just a lunch date," Sallie says.

Those are the worst kind. You only have an hour so besides a meal, any form of entertainment is out of the question. Sallie goes to lunch at noon, which is the exact time the rest of the city goes to lunch too. A nice sit-down restaurant where the waiter comes to your table and hands you a menu is out of the question too, and Sallie isn't dressed for a place like that anyway.

So, they will probably resort to fast food. Sallie will order a diet soda and a side salad consisting only of some wilted lettuce and a slice of tomato. Charlie will order a greasy burger with a large side of fries. They'll chat about their likes and dislikes and discover they have nothing in common. Or they'll find out they have everything in common. It'll be the best date ever, one that Sallie will record in great detail in her diary when she gets home after work. She'll even swipe his straw wrapper or a napkin to press between the pages as a memento. That's what is so bad about such unplanned and sporadic first dates that actually work out. Who wants to spend your whole life with someone and look back one day and remember that first meal you shared together was a greasy burger and a side salad?

"These days, that's all the time you need," Sallie says, "I'll definitely know by the end of lunch if I want to ever see him again."

And that's exactly why I don't date! Unbeknownst to Charlie, he'd have one hour to impress Sallie if he wanted a second date. What if Charlie felt the same way about Sallie? Sallie would be putting forth no effort whatsoever to pique his interest, waiting for him to grab her attention instead. Both would end up thinking the other is a total bore and have their eyes glued to the clock anxious for the lunch hour to be over. When in reality, each one of them could have been the perfect match for the other, but they'd never know it.

Relationships are more like coffee than we'd expect. Sweet. Strong. Dark and bitter.

Nine

The morning was a usual blur because we were so busy. Before either of us knew it we had made it to the breather. The breather is what we call that short period of time after the morning rush finally dies down but before the lunch crowd starts coming in. It doesn't last very long, but it gives Sallie enough time to restock the pastry case before she goes to lunch.

She also usually empties the register and makes a midday deposit, but today she puts the till in a bag and takes it to the safe in the office because of her date with Charlie. I make fresh coffee and wipe down the counters, and make a quick sweep of the prep area with a broom. We have been so busy before, and so clumsy, that the floor behind the counter becomes painted in a gooey mashed mix of coffee grounds, milk, and pastry crumbs. It pays to invest in cheap shoes for this job.

Auden, the only other employee at The Latte Da, arrives at noon to relieve Sallie for lunch. He works the afternoon with me behind the counter, leaving Sallie to run errands or do paperwork in the office. Auden is somewhat of a typical coffeehouse punk kid, only older. He has skillet black greased hair spiked with a twist of purple in the front. Sometimes it's blue or pink. Both ears are pierced several times, and I speculate that other body parts may be too.

His forearms are covered in a fairytale of tattoos. Quite literally. There's Little Red Riding Hood being chased by the Big Bad Wolf; Humpty Dumpty sitting on a wall surrounded by knights on horses, and an array of other Grimm characters all connected by a winding beanstalk that seems to grow out of one knuckle reaching all the way up his arm and under his shirt. His wardrobe on any day consists of only black and white colors, leather boots, and a wallet on a long chain.

At first, he scared me. Anyone brave enough to step outside of society and to step into public looking like Auden quickly gains a reputation of either being a Satan worshiper or a punk rocking druggie. Auden is neither. He has a degree from the local art school and is well versed in literature. Sallie believes he brings a certain flare to the shop that boring people like us lack, and Auden is quite reliable. She trusts him enough to close the shop down by himself in the evenings. He also keeps the evening business going which usually consists of other colorful punk kids just like him.

The Latte Da is like some odd bar that has eccentric after hour parties that no one knows about. We don't advertise them. Patrons only hear about them by word of mouth. There's a gay bar on Madison like that. From seven to midnight, it's a dive bar playing Melissa Etheridge on the jukebox with middle-age lesbians playing pool or pinball. There's a sixty-something retired butch, who likes to write poetry and hosts cook-outs, serving beer on tap behind the bar.

But somewhere between eleven and midnight, the lesbians have all gone home and the entire bar changes. The overhead yellowing lights are dimmed and neon lights flicker. A mirror ball drops out of the ceiling and the jukebox is unplugged. The thump-thump-thump of techno music vibrates speakers overhead. The pool table is lowered into a pit, now concealed beneath a dance floor with tiles that light up when you step on them. The dyke behind the bar morphs into Duke, a shirtless hunk with a German accent who lets you put tips in his G-string while he shakes martinis. Go-go boys dance in cages suspended from the ceiling!

Okay, so The Latte Da is not quite like that. Our morning patrons are businessmen in suites with cell phones and brief cases, or Moms in track suits who just dropped the kids off at school and are on their way to aerobics class or to meet a girlfriend for tennis. Everyone is on the go! Stay-at-home Moms struggle getting strollers in the door or hold up the line trying to invent a sweet concoction for their four year old. Junior is destroying the condiment counter while Mom snaps her fingers at him and threatens to count to three. Sallie gets pissed and blows hair out of her eyes while watching Junior make a picnic blanket on the floor out of paper napkins. I pour the kid milk.

"I wish you had a kid's menu," the snooty bitch says with

a roll of the eyes.

"I wish you had a sign on the door saying NO KIDS ALLOWED," the man behind her quips out loud to us.

My thoughts exactly.

Sallie and I just glance at each other and laugh to ourselves.

By noon when Auden arrives, the line has slowed down and the tables are filled with medical students on laptops. Good-hearted old men sit in the window and read their morning paper. The cheese danishes and cherry cream struddles are almost gone. Sallie replaces them with cornbread muffins and fresh baked cookies. We serve a different soup each day for the small lunch crowd. A black preacher comes in everyday just for the soup, and to sit in the back and prepare his sermons.

By 5pm, the boring students have all gone to class and the old men have taken the bus to Bingo. Students from the art college meander in with portfolios filled with canvases under their arms. Each knows Auden by name. They nibble cookies and leftover bagels, and sip soy lattes and caramel mochas. They push the tables together to set up shop and sketch drawings with an array of colored pencils and oil crayons thrown across the table. Others hang out in the overstuffed chairs and chat about the project they were assigned in pottery class that day, eagerly seeking the opinion of their peers. They are a young crowd, too young to get into bars and too smart to smoke cigarettes. They have dreams of becoming furniture designers and graphic artists.

Laced in the fads of the day, they all share things in common but each is different. The first year students wear tennis shoes and rubber friendship bracelets. Second and third year wear dark eye shadow and bright red lipstick, both the boys and the girls. Fourth year students have facial hair and wear khakis with cotton shirts. And they've probably been fourth year students for at least two or three years now, clinging to the acceptance that only other creative students like them can provide.

"They become their art," Auden says, "and as they progress their art changes."

"And so do they?" I ask.

"Exactly."

"What were you like your first year of college?"

"I've always been this way."

I felt like Auden was hiding something, like a painter who paints a picture on a stretched canvas but is dissatisfied with it and paints over it. Only he knows what's underneath. I wish I knew.

Ten

Auden restocks the straws, napkins, and stirrers when he arrives. I've finished my mid-day prep work behind the counter so I go over to help him. Sallie has removed her apron and gone to the restroom to "freshen up" before her date arrives. She's done a good job of keeping calm all day. On the inside, I know she has been a nervous wreck and is probably now pacing the restroom or trying to look a bit more appealing by applying what little makeup she keeps in her purse.

"Sallie has a date," I tell Auden.

"What? With who?"

"Some guy named Charlie who she met outside when she came to work this morning. He's supposed to be picking her up shortly."

"Outside in front of the café? There are only homeless people outside that early in the morning."

"That's where she told me they met. Just this morning," I say. I respect the way Auden calls this place a *café*.

"They are going to lunch together? Today?"

"Yep. He'll be here any minute. She told me to let her know when he comes in."

"What is she thinking?"

"I don't know, but she's in the restroom now preparing herself."

"Preparing for doom is more like it. Spur of the minute dates like that never work out. Never!"

I half expect her to emerge from the restroom looking like some effeminate boy who snuck into Mommy's bureau. Sallie has scorching red hair and pale freckled skin, and she is actually quite eye-catching with little make-up on at all if any. The cosmetics in her purse consist mainly of free samples handed to her by mall clerks just trying to push a product, or some cherry red lipstick and blue eye shadow leftover from playing a hooker on Halloween two years ago.

As if the heavens are in our favor, the only couple in the

shop gets up to leave. I nod at them with a thank-you and rush over and dust crumbs off their table. I glance around to make sure everything looks orderly as if Charlie was a potential investor who we want to impress. I just pray that we don't get a sudden rush of customers before he comes in because I want to meet him. Auden and I both will size him up, smile to his face, and then talk bad about him once they leave.

Our backs are to the door as we finish with the condiment counter. I glance up at the clock above the cash register and notice it's one minute till noon. Suddenly, the door chimes behind us and we both turn in unison to see who is coming in. Just after a quick glance we turn back to one another, eyes bulging in disbelief.

Eleven

"Hi. I'm here to pick up Sallie. Is she around?"

Before me stands a young business man in an expensive suit, but he seems very relaxed in his attire as if he probably wore it every day. He was no different than any lawyer or real estate agent that walks through the door every morning for a hot beverage, except that Charlie was quite striking in appearance. He had neat blond hair that was short with high-lights and deep blue eyes that gave me goose bumps when I looked in them.

He was a bit shorter than me in stature, but probably the same height as Sallie. His shoulders and chest were broad beneath his crisp shirt and polo jacket, so he obviously spent time at the gym. His skin was evenly tanned and without a single blemish. His shoes were shiny and polished; there was an expensive gold watch gleaming on his wrist. He was the epitome of either new money or the beneficiary of daddy's fortune.

"Sure, can I tell her who is here?" I ask.

"I'm Charlie."

"Hi, I'm Blaine."

Charlie extends a hand and we shake. It's a firm handshake that almost hurts. I stand in front of him for a second, lost in some trance and rubbing the immediate soreness of my palm brought about by his grasp. He smiles and twitches his eyebrows, probably calling me some rude name beneath his breath.

"Sallie will be out in just a minute," Auden calls from the door to the stock room in an attempt to snap me out of my hypnotic state.

I smile and nod at Charlie to dismiss myself and then rush to the stock room.

"Well, what do you think?" Auden asks.

"He's gorgeous. I can't believe it."

"What? You can't believe that someone like him would be interested in Sallie?"

"Exactly."

"Why not? Opposites attract," Auden says.

I don't really believe that. People only say opposites attract to hide the fact that they have nothing in common with the person they ended up with. If dating was perfect, we'd all want to be with a clone of ourselves. That is, unless we absolutely hate everything about ourselves. If so, then we are destined to end up with someone who absolutely loves everything about themselves. The opposite!

But what does Auden know. I think he claims to be bisexual too, but he probably hasn't dated anyone seriously since high school. He probably takes out personal ads in both the men seeking men and men seeking women columns. Maybe he goes on blind dates, and he's even tried those dating hotlines they advertise on television. I don't know.

So, what's his real excuse? I've never asked, but I imagine he'd reply by saying something profound like, "I just haven't found Mr. Right, or Mrs."

Notice I put Mister first. His preference, perhaps? I don't really know. I've never looked at Auden that way, or really wondered about his personal life outside of the coffee shop.

There's a back door in the stockroom that we keep locked that leads into both restrooms. I knock on it to let Sallie know that Charlie has arrived. She doesn't answer so I call out to her, "Charlie's here!"

"Five bucks says he's a lawyer," Auden says.

"I was thinking real estate."

"Maybe a doctor?"

"Nah, doctors wear scrubs or lab coats to work. If he was going on a lunch date, he wouldn't change into a suit."

"True, but what kind of businessman calls himself Charlie? Wouldn't he say his name is Charles if he wanted to seem so professional?"

"Good point."

"Maybe he's an accountant then?"

"Again, why the suit?"

"Maybe he's head of his own accounting firm," Auden says.

"He's a professor," Sallie says from behind us, finally emerging from the restroom like a beauty queen who just stepped on stage.

She looks radiant. Her hair is pinned back. Her complexion is warm, not painted, with just the right amount of make-up. Her white shirt is tucked beneath her skirt, with no remnants of frosting or powdered sugar lingering down the front. She's even rolled the skirt up a bit to show some leg. A piece of cloth from a Christmas window display is tied around her waist as a scarf.

This is the Sallie I once knew. It's the Sallie that used to get up early in the morning to fix her hair in hopes that Mr. Right would walk into the shop that day. It's the Sallie that would laugh above the crowd at the bar and toss her hair to get a guy's attention, the Sallie that would bat her eyes at customers who left good tips. This Sallie was fun. She's always been fun, even after she gave up and stopped caring, after she stopped looking like this every day. This Sallie went dormant and the single, middle-aged lonely Sallie materialized. And it seems that Sallie I once knew has just been hiding in the restroom all this time.

"A professor of what?" Auden asks.

I'm speechless, still amazed at how she turned that tree skirt into a sash.

"English literature. At the university," She says, "Well, how do I look?"

She does a turn and giggles. It's a giggle I haven't heard in years.

"You look great," Auden says.

"What do you think of Charlie?" She asks.

"He's hot. You're hot. Look at you, Sallie," Auden says with a grin.

"Well, Blaine, aren't you going to say anything?" Sallie asks.

She slaps me on the cheek bringing me back.

"What?" I shake my head.

"Aren't you going to say anything?"

"I'd fuck him!"

It's the first thought that blurts out of my mouth. I'm so embarrassed, but Auden and Sallie just laugh.

"Not until I've had him first," she coos.

And like that, she sashays out the stock room door and greets Charlie with a smile. He looks her up and down and smiles with approval, giving her a compliment. Like parents standing at the window who just met the boyfriend for the first time, Auden and I watch as he offers our girl his arm and opens the door for her. He ushers her down the sidewalk and they fade into the afternoon light.

"Wow, it's like a fairy tale," Auden exclaims.

"Do you have this one tattooed on you as well?"

"Prince Charming and Sleeping Beauty. Between my shoulder blades."

Auden raises his shirt and I admire his picture book back before going back to work. The vivid memory of his inked skin coats my brain like a fascinating day dream. I wish I could have touched it.

Twelve

Sallie calls later and asks if it's okay with us if she takes the rest of the afternoon off. I assume that it's because she's actually having a good time, not because she's absolutely humiliated and wants to avoid having to face us to regurgitate the horrid details of her lunch date.

"Do you want me to stay to help you close?" I ask Auden at the end of my shift.

"No, I'll be fine. Go enjoy the rest of your afternoon."

"I guess we'll have to wait till tomorrow for all the details, huh?"

"I'm sure she's having a wonderful time. She deserves to, at least."

"Yeah. Call me if she stops back by."

With Sallie, I would cherish every detail if they were good or bad. I'd eagerly cling to each revolting comment she'd make about Charlie with my mouth dropped open and the occasional elongated "Noooo!" I'd hug her when she breaks down and starts to cry, begging me not to say I told her so. I'd rest easy that night like a tucked-in kid satisfied with a bedtime story.

Instead, if her particulars turned into the "best date I ever had" essay, I'd listen attentively just the same because she appreciates the quality that I'm a good listener. She trusts me. In the end, I'd still hug her but congratulatory-like with a soft pat on the back and then roll my eyes in disgust over her shoulder just glad that the love story was finally over.

Jealousy? You betcha.

"Are you going to the park today?" Auden asks.

"I think so."

Auden relates to my interest in photography because of his love of art. Photography was one aspect that he says he barely touched on in college though. He doesn't understand the mechanics of a camera, the functions of its parts and their effect on the shot. He prefers a blank canvas, a selection of paints and brushes; he wants to create something out of his mind rather than capture something real in the moment. He appreciates the fact that art is all around us. It's just the interpretation of that art that makes Auden and me different.

Opposites.

Thirteen

Bachardy Park is exactly 32 blocks from the coffee shop, but that's not the foremost reason I go there. It's actually the smallest park in the city, nestled between two downtown skyscrapers encompassing one small city block. There are condominiums on one side and a large banking corporation on the other. Hectic one way streets run parallel on the other two sides bustling with honking buses, yellow cabs, and inner-city pedestrians.

I'm amazed that some urban planner spared it. But I guess that amidst the concrete walls and parking meters, the city needed some green. The herb trees neglected on narrow window sills of the expensive condos or fake plants in offices and lobbies just weren't enough.

The trees in Bachardy Park are so tall, unlike any others I've seen before, and there is one at each corner of the park. When you sit in the park beneath the trees and look up, their branches intertwine like a mad picture frame and block out the buildings around them. Directly in the middle, there is only sky, a bit of blue sky. If you are lucky enough to be there at the right time of day the sun shines down through the gap in the trees onto a pigeon fountain directly in the middle of the park.

The fountain is two stories tall and divided into three tiers with a statue of some angelic woman at the top. She stands in the middle of an ornate spigot with water billowing out from her feet in a starburst spray and falling into the smaller basin beneath her, then pouring over the sides into the large basin at the foundation. Her arms are stretched upward and she too is looking toward the sky.

Unlike many grand statues of angels with their wings outstretched wider than their arms, this angel's wings are tiny and cannot even be seen from the front of her. It's as if neither her wings nor the lifting pressure of the water could raise her from this ground. Maybe she climbed up the fountain to reach higher ground but just gave up and stayed there. Hopeless.

Pigeons bobble on her shoulders and strut on the edge of the basins. A coppery reflection envelops the marble folds of her gown from all of the pennies tossed in on wishes, including a few of my own. I have snapped many a picture of her, but I let her hide from my camera lens today.

The tiny fortune that lies in the rippling water below her has always intrigued me. I've watched many young, and old, couples stand at the iron barrier around the basin, the man digging in his pocket for a coin. He gives a penny or a nickel to the girl to toss in and make a wish. Maybe he throws in a coin too. Neither asks what the other wished for, but they hug like they already know.

Maybe she wished he'd ask for her hand in marriage. Maybe she wished he'd die so she wouldn't have to break up with him. Maybe he wished he'd get laid tonight. It's all like someone blowing out the candles on their birthday cake. It is supposedly taboo for anyone to ask what they wished for because then it might not come true. I still always want to ask them, but I don't.

Instead, after the couple embrace and stroll on through the park, I check to make sure no one is looking. Then, I reach over the barrier and dip my hand into the cold water. I take a penny or a nickel off the bottom and keep it. It goes in a jar I keep in the top of my bedroom closet. Call me a thief but maybe—just maybe—I'm a savior to some. I don't know if stealing someone's wishes keeps them from coming true or not.

But I wish I knew.

There are five benches that encircle the park facing inward and one more positioned next to each of the four trees and facing outward. Each time I come to the park, I sit on a different bench and observe. Quite passive, recording, not thinking, as Isherwood put it. I examine the outlook from each bench as if I am in a totally different place, although each view is just a small piece of the overall larger picture.

I may capture an old man with a cane just passing through, or a condo dweller walking their dog, or a young lady with an umbrella. I could shoot them with the camera from any direction, from any bench in the park, and it wouldn't change who they are. Only the background would change, where they are in the park changes. The tree limbs in the background are different sizes, or we see the side of the fountain instead of the front. The angel is looking to the right or her back is turned. I can turn the camera right side up or long ways creating a whole new position within a location. And so is life.

We can't change who we are, only where we are. So, I try not to obsess about it.

Fourteen

Although the fountain is the focal point of the park, to one corner there is a round concrete pavement nestled in the middle of some bushes. It's like an empty wading pool and even holds water in the middle for a few days after a rain. Maybe it was the base of a pavilion years ago where a quartet once played, or served as a patio for park goers to have some shade back before the trees grew so tall. Its lid shaped surface reminds me of a landing pad for some strange aircraft, or maybe it's a large secret manhole that leads to an underground world that we are all just supposed to ignore.

These days it serves as the spot for a street vendor who sells fresh popcorn and roasted peanuts, most of which are bought and fed to pigeons and squirrels in the park. Today, I have the park to myself except for an older lady with a young girl tugging at the bottom of her coat. She buys a box of popcorn and hands it to the little girl. The girl turns and runs toward a nearby park bench, directly across the way from me. The older lady, buying a bag of peanuts, calls out for the little girl to slow down.

I watch this innocent occurrence through the eye of my camera, unnoticed by the little girl and her elderly guardian. The little girl sits her box of popcorn down on the pavement as she climbs up onto the bench. A brave frisky squirrel pops out of the bushes and runs under the bench to nab a kernel of popcorn that has fallen to the ground. His bushy tail tickles the girl's small legs as she teeters on and off the bench like she's trying to mount a pony. Not seeing the squirrel, she lets go of the bench to rub her leg, loses her balance and falls to the ground spilling the box of popcorn.

By now, I've started shooting pictures continuously ever since the squirrel drew near. The old lady turns to see what is happening when the little girl lets out a small cry. Popcorn scatters across the ground, and like magic a flock of at least two dozen pigeons flies down from the trees engulfing the little girl and rapidly eating up the popcorn. She screams again from all the flapping of wings. The old lady rushes over, shooing the fearless pigeons so she can get to the child and help her up, but the little girl is already on her feet.

The girl laughs at the funny grey and white birds and reaches for what's left of the popcorn. She grabs the box and throws the rest of the kernels up into the air. Her sudden movement startles the birds and they fly away in an explosion of feathers. With her hands in the air as if she had just freed all of the pigeons from a cage, the little girl beams with a wide smile all captured on film. The old lady smiles, probably wishing she had a camera.

It is a pure and candid moment like this that reminds me why I like Bachardy Park so much and why I like to take pictures. It is a special individual moment that both the little girl and the old lady will stash away in their memory for a long time to come, just as I will paste the 4 x 6 glossy recollections between the pages of one of my scrapbooks to recall one day as well.

Fifteen

In today's society, convenience has overridden quality in just about everything but coffee. Coffeehouses are where convenience and distinction merge almost semi-appropriately. People still care about the quality of a good coffee drink, but I think we are the last coffeehouse in town that still makes its customers park and walk inside to place their order. Sallie hates drive-through windows because they aren't very personable, so she avoids the conversation every time a customer brings it up. Food and drink should be just as much about the visual as it is the taste, so Sallie likes people to have to come inside and see the pastry case and smell the aroma of fresh ground coffee. You lose that when you are ordering from a sign and yelling into a box of static from your car window at the back of the building with a view of their trash receptacles.

It's the same in the society of cameras and picture taking. No one uses 35 millimeter anymore, and I can't tell you the last time I bought a roll of film. It's all about digital downloading and memory cards. Cameras have also gotten smaller (for convenience) because people are always on the go and just have time for snapshots. They even build cameras into cell phones these days that claim to be able to take quality pictures, but I don't believe them. I think these "conveniences" have just changed our sense of quality overtime. We are more pleased with the ability to carry a camera in our pocket so that we don't miss that Kodak moment, rather than being prepared with the right equipment to take a meaningful and quality photo.

And there is some truth to that because what is the one thing you always forget when you are going on a picnic or a quick road trip? The camera. But we are hardly ever without our cell phones, so the camera problem is solved for us. We don't have to remember the camera from now on. But I'm always the one who does remember to bring the camera.

And I loathe those small easy one-click snapshot digital pocket cameras. Again, those were designed for convenience but totally overlook quality. Ninety percent of the people who go shopping for cameras probably tell the salesman they want something convenient. And he probably makes a whopping commission for selling them some piece of crap keychain camera with a 3X zoom. The customer buys it and wastes three hundred dollars on the tiny pill box piece of shit because they think it's so cute and they are amazed at how it fits right in the palm of their hand. The salesman even shows them some top quality photos taken with that very camera, which he shows to every customer, even though those pictures were not even taken with a camera sold in that store!

I do appreciate the convenience of digital cameras for the mere fact of being able to upload the pictures to my computer as soon as I get home. Unlike the old days where you went to the photo counter in your local drug store and put your film in an envelope to be sent off and developed, and you came back and picked up your photos two weeks later. How could anyone bear the anticipation! And then when you picked the photos up, you were disappointed at over half of the roll because your subjects either have red eyes, or the flash reflected in a mirror, or your thumb got in the shot. At least with a digital camera you can see the mistakes instantly and hopefully have a better chance of correcting them. So, I believe the camera industry has even found a way to improve the quality of our memories, or at least the photogenic recording of them.

My digital camera is not one of those snapshot matchboxes, but rather a heftier digital with all the buttons and whistles, a higher resolution zoom and a selection of photo-taking options from sepia colored photos to black and white. It has a large black leather strap and hangs around my neck like any father's old clunky 35 millimeter, but at least it feels like a camera when grasped firmly in my hands, not some plastic kid's palm-sized camera that breaks if you push the button too hard.

It's the only camera I own. Remember, I am a novice and certainly not one of those people so absorbed in their hobby that they need to surround themselves with the paraphernalia needed to do it. Photo-taking is not like collecting baseball cards where you continue to search for and buy more and more, at least I don't think so. I feel the need to only have one good camera, not several. After all, the camera produces the end result of the keystone of my hobby itself. The photos.

It's the photos that make up the better part of my pastime. Sure, the fundamental nature and the moment of setting up for the photo is part of the anticipation, but you don't always get that. That's why I like sitting in the park and just being in the moment, continuously waiting for that perfect snapshot to happen. I sit and remain poised, camera in hand and positioned to a good setting depending on the sun or the shadows of the trees that day. And life just happens, naturally and not posed.

Most days nothing happens. Maybe no one is in the park that day but me. All I end up with is a photo of a pigeon in the fountain or a tree root that catches my eye, and a handful of wishes.

But that's the quality of life. People aren't always in the picture. So why obsess about it?

Sixteen

Beep...beep...beep...

I'm up at 5:32am on time as usual. Today is a cold cereal day. I leave at 6:32am but today I do a light jog to work in hopes of arriving eight minutes earlier than my usual early time so that Sallie can begin telling me about her date. I'm shocked to find Auden drizzling icing on scones instead of Sallie.

"She called last night and asked if I would open for her," Auden explains when I get inside.

"Why didn't she call me?"

"I guess she didn't want to mess up your schedule."

"She could have at least called me just to let me know she wasn't going to be here. She could have told me about the date. Did she tell you about the date?"

"No."

"You're lying."

"No, I'm not."

"What did she say?"

"Not much. She said she had a good time and that they had a late night—"

"And?"

"And she had a little too much to drink and wanted to sleep in this morning. So, she asked if I would cover for her and I said yes. Would you like to know anything else, Blaine?"

"I still don't know why she didn't call me."

"I wouldn't worry about it. Like she said, she just didn't want to mess up your morning schedule."

"What about you? What about your morning schedule?"

"I don't have a morning schedule. I get up with the chickens and watch television all morning until time to come to work."

"I didn't know you had chickens."

"I don't. It's a figure of...oh, never mind!"

Auden goes back to arranging the pastry case while I make the coffee and prep the espresso machine. I remain quiet through most of the morning rush because my thoughts are on Sallie's actions. I wonder if she is just keeping something from me. I'd like to think that I'm a closer friend of hers than Auden is. She never even hangs out with Auden and she tells me everything. At least I thought she told me everything. Maybe she actually tells Auden instead, and he is just lying to me. But I don't think Auden would lie. What if she does tell Auden all the good stuff, and all this time I thought she only told me? So the things she has told me, which I thought were the good stuff, are actually all lies or just fluff. Maybe Sallie leads an alternative life that I know nothing about.

I wonder if the date with Charlie was so embarrassing and awkward that she couldn't accept coming back to work to face us, so she took the rest of the day off. She woke up this morning still mortified over how much of a waste of time the date was, so she just needed the time off to recover. Or what if Charlie smacked her around? What if she has a black eye and couldn't bear to be seen at work and have to explain everything to me?

The work day slowly slides by and not once does the phone ring. I check the door every single time the bell chimes announcing someone coming in or leaving, hoping to see Sallie walk in but she never comes. I offer to stay late to help Auden close down, but he assures me that he'll be fine. He knows that my mind has been preoccupied all day, and truthfully he's probably ready for me to leave by now. I really didn't want to stay late anyway, and knew he probably wouldn't ask me to.

All day, I've been wondering if I should call Sallie myself. By the end of my shift I decide that I'm going to leave work and go over to her apartment instead, half expecting to find her tied to the bed helpless or something even worse. She might be dead. I walk to her apartment, which just so happens to be sixteen blocks from the coffeehouse and another sixteen blocks from my own apartment. You do the math.

I knock lightly on the door. No answer. I knock again but louder. And then I hear her voice.

"Just a minute."

She sounds chipper for a woman who has probably just

had the absolute nastiest time of her life, so bad that she couldn't face the work day or her coworkers, or even her best friend.   I hear the sound of high heels clicking on the kitchen tile as she comes to the door. *She never wears heels*, I think to myself. The door opens.

"Blaine, what are you doing here?" Sallie asks.

Seventeen

There is a certain glow that people emit when they are satisfied sexually. I think it's much easier to detect in women than in men. With men, the deed is done and they roll over and fall asleep or get up and put their clothes on and leave. The women lie secretly awake, maybe even nestled in the arms of their lover, and allow the transformation to take place. In the morning, they wake up a brand new female, giving resounding meaning to whoever said, "This is the first day of the rest of your life." Sallie obviously is no exception.

She stands before me in a white satin slip nightgown of some kind with spaghetti straps and lots of cleavage. That's another thing about women too. They may not have a private top drawer of special lingerie that their friends are aware of, but when the time is appropriate sexy underwear always magically appears. The same goes for gay men and hot underwear except that we usually wear ours all the time instead of saving it for special occasions.

Sallie is indeed wearing heels. They are white with a three inch heel and a feathery poof on the top. Very sexy. Her hair is a mess and somehow mysteriously grew about six inches over night, tousled over her shoulders like a beauty queen. She wears it pinned back at work and when we go out, so I had no idea just how much hair she actually had. Maybe she's been saving it for a special occasion too.

To complete the ensemble, there's a wine glass in her hand and I feel as though I should have to pay her before I come inside her apartment. I refrain from any prostitution jokes. I'd almost mistaken her demeanor for intoxication, but I know that it is something completely different. Sallie got laid.

"Can I come in?"

"Of course." She steps aside and lets me enter.

"Are you alone?"

"Oh honey, would I let you in if I wasn't?"

"I just wanted to stop in and check on you since I haven't

heard from you today," I say stressing my last few words to make a point.

"Sorry about that," she says wrinkling her face. "I didn't want to mess up your schedule."

"It's okay. Soooo, are you going to tell me?"

"Tell you what?" She asks with a giggle.

"Sallie, don't make me beg!"

"Oh, you mean tell you about Charlie?" She teases.

"Details!"

She pours a glass of wine for me and refills her own. She sits on her sofa with her legs stretched out, heels still on. I sit in the adjacent chair with my legs crossed, like a psychiatrist eager to hear the patient's woes of the day, but by now I think her story will be anything but despair.

Charlie took her to Berlin. Not the country, but a German restaurant downtown on the river. Surprisingly, it's a place where neither of us had been before. Charlie ordered Herring Fillets in Wine Sauce and Sallie had Apple Herring in a Mustard Sauce. She had never eaten herring before and couldn't pronounce anything else on the menu besides bratwursts. Charlie ordered caviar as an appetizer for them along with a bottle of imported wine. Each dining booth was completely private and candle lit. They skipped the German dessert and opted to take a leisurely stroll through downtown along the river walk. Since Charlie was new in town, he had not seen much of the city. He was excited to have his own personal tour guide of downtown.

Charlie just moved here from California at the beginning of the semester and is the head of the English department at the University. He is also teaching two English lit courses, and directing a couple of students with getting their masters. He's never married and his last long-term relationship was over four years ago. It lasted two and half years and supposedly ended because the girl moved overseas to teach English as a second language.

Sallie and Charlie were enjoying each other's company so much that they decided to go have dessert after all. They walked back to an ice cream shop they had passed outside the restaurant and ordered a banana split with two spoons. By now, they were both pleasantly enjoying each other's company and weren't ready for the date to end. Charlie had the rest of the afternoon off, and Sallie decided to take the rest of the day off as well. Sallie admitted that several times throughout the date she had come to a loss for words just from looking deep into Charlie's stunning eyes. They were so mesmerizing that it was as if she was lost in a daydream. Some facial feature of hers must have had the same effect on him because Charlie would blush when he snapped back from the silence.

Charlie asked Sallie if she would like to accompany him to a jazz bar that night where a small band that he liked was performing. Of course, she said yes. He dropped her off at her apartment and agreed to pick her up in an hour, giving her a chance to change clothes. Charlie went home to change out of his suit and into more casual clothing. He knocked on her door right on time wearing perfect fitting jeans and a red pullover. Sallie had changed into jeans and a sweater, and unpinned her hair.

The band was playing at a bar called Mr. Norris's, another place that Sallie and I had surprisingly never been to before but had always wanted to go. They shared a few bottles of champagne at a small table in the corner all night. They both paid attention to the band during their first set, then when the band took a break Sallie people-watched couples on the dance floor. Charlie watched Sallie and when she turned, feeling the weight of his glance, he kissed her. His lips were soft and his kisses were firm. She melted into the curve of his body with the verbiage of a romance novel. When their third bottle of champagne went dry, Charlie was fumbling for his car keys.

Sallie pretty much left the rest of the evening up to my imagination. I pictured any Hollywood love scene where the door is practically knocked down as they struggle with each other's clothing. Lamps and tables are knocked over in the dark. Clothing is thrown to the floor. Panties are ripped, beads of sweat form, and bed sheets are scrunched. Breathless sounds of lovemaking echo through her apartment all night. They collapse

in exhausted kisses after hours of nonstop lovemaking.
It made me throw up just a little in my mouth.

Eighteen

Days would pass with Sallie not mentioning Charlie, but I knew she had seen him practically every night. It's not uncommon for anyone to have a new beau and keep him all to themselves for a while. It's like a kid hiding Easter candy long after the holiday is gone. We are thrilled by the undivided attention. We don't have to listen to our friends' opinions. We don't have to worry about his judgment of our friends. But sooner or later, the bloom rubs off.

We've settled in. The new toy isn't as shiny anymore. Most gay men wish they had a new toy by now. Women miss their friends and decide it's finally time to mix the best friend-boyfriend cocktail to see what happens. Most gay men will skip right to this step. They'll meet and bed a guy on Friday, and be kissing him on the dance floor on Saturday. They want everyone to see their trophy. They want to be admired, even hated at the expense of seeming cheap.

Years ago, I'd be guilty of the same thing but there comes a time in life when we outgrow the Easter parade. We want to settle down, but still want it to be exciting. Remember being courted in high school and walking each other to your lockers, writing each other notes in class, sitting together at lunch, wearing each other's class rings? These day kids just text each other on their cell phones and send emails across the lunchroom. Gay men don't have all that, unless they want to risk being the brunt of all the jokes in the locker room at gym class, so by the time high school ends we have a lot of catching up to do. Maybe that's why gay men sleep with everyone.

Women are different but still demand the same type of attention throughout life. They want to be courted. And I can't think of any woman who deserves it more than Sallie. So I don't say anything. She may secretly wish that I would ask her about how things are going with Charlie, but I rather like building the suspense. I know the time will come when she can't stand it any longer and she'll want to go to dinner one night to tell me everything.

For now, they must be keeping the midnight oil burning. Sallie arrives at work everyday with her hair and makeup fixed. Her clothes are ironed. And she either went shopping for new clothes or excavated the back corners of her closet because she is wearing new outfits I don't think I've ever seen before. She pauses sometimes in the middle of a task as if she might fall asleep; then she snaps out of it with a giggle. She laughs to herself obviously replaying the events of last night's bedtime story in her head.

"What's so funny?" Auden or I will ask.

"Oh, nothing. It's nothing," she answers.

Auden and I roll our eyes and leave it at that.

About two weeks pass, and Sallie is ready to play bartender. I can tell because not only does she remain quiet all morning, but she also seems hesitant. It's as if she is trying to figure out how to ask me to borrow some money. But I know that she is just working the conversation out in her head on how she's going to ask me to accompany her and Charlie to a ball game, or a movie night, or dinner at his place.

"Do you want to go to lunch today?" She asks halfway through the morning rush.

"That sounds great!"

She smiles. The tension in the air clears.

She knows that no matter what she asks me to do with them, I'll say yes. Well, almost anything. I wouldn't do anything weird like take photos of them in bed together. Okay, if she offered to pay me, I might say yes to that.

No! No, definitely not! She'd never ask me to do that anyway.

But I'd say yes to anything else.

Nineteen

"No!"

"Why not, Blaine?"

"Absolutely not! No way!"

Sallie treats me to lunch at a deli we both love. The food is a bit expensive, but the portions make it worth every penny. The boys behind the counter make for some nice eye candy too in their tight white tees, jeans, and black aprons. We sit down to eat and she butters me up by asking me how *I'm* doing.

Now when someone who you work with, who you've seen practically every day for the past eight years of your life, suddenly sits down and wants to know how *you* are doing, they are really giving you a chance to clear the air. It's quite possible that they've somehow become the center of attention for quite some time, like Sallie has, and now here's your opportunity to catch them up on your boring life. What she is really doing is giving me time to talk about me, to put the focus on me. It's my chance to shine right here at the table, to put the spotlight on me and say, "Hey, look at me for a while!"

It's really a cheap ploy to ask me for a favor. Sallie should know by now that I've never wanted to be in the spotlight. I'll do anything possible to avoid the attention of others. I prefer the back row. There's nothing exciting or glamorous happening in my life that she's missed out on since she met Charlie. It's kind to stop and let someone else talk about themselves for a while though. Everyone has a story to tell. And I guess proper etiquette is to pass the torch when you are done and let the other person talk back a while. Chances are they have something even better to say, but you better step up and take the mike when the floor is open to you. And so I do. I tell her about the child in the park and the photo I took.

You see, Sallie is the one person who understands me and the photos I take. She gets it. Besides Auden, there really isn't anyone in my life worth showing my photos to. It's a lot like showing your recent vacation photos to coworkers. You get lots of "oohs" and "ahhs" and "that's nice," but once you put the photos away no one really cares. They care more about you returning to work to catch up on your job than anything else. But I can see in Sallie's eyes that it's different. She knows what that photo means to me. She shares in my excitement of being in that very moment. She understands. And that's why I trust her.

I don't have the photo with me to show her, but she expresses interest in seeing it. I have nothing else to talk about so I ask how things are going with Charlie. She knew that I eventually would, and that opened the floor for her to ask for the favor I already know she wants from me. I know that at first I'll say no. I don't want to be a third wheel. But it's possible that Charlie has already bought three tickets to whatever event needs to be the ice breaker between her best friend and her boyfriend. She'll beg a little. I'll let her. Then of course, I'll pretend to give in and say I'm doing it just for her, knowing that I would say yes all the time. But that's not what happened. That's not what she asked at all.

"Blaine, just tell me why not?"

"I said no!"

At some point during her time spent with Charlie, Sallie had to discuss her friends, those other people in her life that she paid attention to before he came into the picture. Over a drink at dinner or a bowl of popcorn on the sofa, they each rambled through their lists of friends, family, and coworkers. They skipped the boring ones that neither of them will probably meet anyway, and traded descriptions of the more colorful bunch. I guess that's one plus to being the token gay friend. People are always going to talk about you when they are telling others about their friends, only Sallie wasn't expecting Charlie's reply the night she played the gay friend card. He had a gay friend too.

And this led to the bright idea that they should plan a blind date between their two gay friends and that all four of us could double date one night. Straight couples don't seem to have a problem with that. They assume because they have two friends who "have something in common" that they will automatically like each other. It's a lot like being friends with a black person and then someone else says to you, "Oh, I have a black friend too!" Blind dates sometimes work out for straight people, but never for gays.

Heterosexuals might meet over dinner and the ladies will excuse themselves to go to the bathroom to find out if the blind girl is into the blind guy or not. If she's not, her girlfriend will protect her through the night and find some way to make sure the two of them are never left alone. She might even spill wine on her dress just so the date can end early. Then, she'll explain it all to her boyfriend at home that night who will have to later tell his unsuspecting friend, "Dude, she just wasn't into you."

But if the girl was into him, that's the easy part. The two couples will just split up at the bar to chat. The blind date couple will go to one corner to get to know each other better, and the matchmaking couple will hit the dance floor to celebrate their triumph. The blind date couple will exchange phone numbers, and he might even kiss her. She'll call her girl friend at home that night and giggle on the phone about how cute he was, how nice he was, and how sincere he was. The guy text messages his friend and tells him he can't wait to get laid.

Blind dates never work out for gay guys, especially when it's going to be a double date with their straight friends! First, there's no excusing myself to go the restroom with Sallie to tell her if I'm into Charlie's friend or not. So, communication becomes a problem. Charlie and his friend are able to go to the can to talk strategy, but what gay guy goes to the bathroom with his straight friend at dinner? And this leads to the next problem. Where do we go after dinner?

If we go to a movie and they let the gay guys sit next to one another, we can't really talk because we're in a movie. So, maybe we go to a bar instead. If we go to a straight bar and couple off, the gay guys can't really talk about the things we want to talk about and be comfortable like we could in a gay bar. But we can't go to a gay bar because that wouldn't be fair to the straight couple that set us up on this horrible date to begin with.

"What if I give him your number and I'll give you his number? Would you call him?"

"No! No, no, no! What part of *no* do you not understand?"

"Blaine, I know you've been angry at me and maybe even a little jealous ever since the lunch date with Charlie. Now, here's the perfect chance for you to meet someone you might like and it took little or no effort on your part. You don't have to do this for me. Do it for yourself."

"I'm not angry," I replied.

"Okay."

"Maybe just a little jealous."

"That's okay too."

I kept my eyes focused on my plate, ignoring Sallie's eyes for a moment. Instead, I admired the perfect layers of my sandwich: bread, meat, cheese, lettuce, tomato, pickle, bread. Each piece of the tasty conundrum was flawlessly in place. In my mind, I traced the edges of the food equation until I came to the spot where I had taken a bite. The shape of my teeth was pressed into the bread, which had already bounced back from the grip of my hand.

We sometimes become too comfortable sitting on a plate of life. The pieces of our puzzle have all been put into place with ease. And then someone comes along and takes a bite out of it.

I'd bounce back.

Twenty

"So, you'll go?" Sallie asked.

"Yes, I'll go. Where will we be going to?"

"We haven't decided. Any ideas?"

"No movies. No bars," I said.

"I thought gay guys liked bars."

"Gay guys like gay bars. Does Charlie like gay bars too?"

"Good point. No bars then."

"Have you seen him?"

"Seen who?"

"My date."

"Oh, yes. His name is Edward. I had dinner with him one night at Charlie's house."

"Is he cute?"

"Does it matter?" Sallie asked, paying the bill.

"Not yet."

"He's very cute. I think you will be pleasantly surprised."

I think I'd be more surprised if he turned out to be a troll. I'd wonder what in the hell was Sallie thinking trying to set me up with some ugly guy like that. I don't want to be surprised. I want to be elated.

"What does he do?" I asked.

"He's a teacher, just like Charlie. They both teach in the English department at the University. Edward teaches creative writing and poetry."

"At least he's smart. But what interest do you think a college professor will have in an obsessive compulsive photo-taking coffee barista?"

"You're both gay. You might get laid?"

"Fair enough."

I wasn't going to debate Sallie. I had already said yes to her plan, and I knew at this point there would be no backing out. I could ask question after question about Edward and she'd only answer with some smart-laced witticism. She's fond of keeping me in suspense. There's always been a bit of mystery to her, and she likes it that way.

So, like an eager eight-year old child unsuccessfully snooping around for plans of a surprise birthday party, I'd be left in the dark until the night of our date. In Sallie's presence, I desperately tried to remain at ease and not phased one bit. But she knew that deep within the clock-like confines of my mind, I was ticking.

Twenty-One

You've probably noticed by now that outside the walls of my apartment I seem pretty normal. My eccentricities are never around when I'm with friends or at work, but believe me, they are still there. I just haven't mentioned them. I'm much more comfortable around people I know and trust, and somehow I have better control over those situations. No, I am not heavily medicated. I wish I was. I probably should be, but shouldn't we all?

I count the thirty-two steps up to the second story and outline the apartment number on my door with my fingers. I trace the three with my left index finger, and trace the two with my right. I do not turn the doorknob thirty-two times before opening it. I may be sick, but I'm not crazy. I push the door open and stand there in the doorway for a few minutes surveying my dark living room.

If I'm going to go on a date, this will require some serious cleaning. Besides Sallie or the property repair man, no one has seen the inside of this apartment in quite a while. I start by changing the light bulbs. None of them are burned out, but I feel the need for new light. Then, I dust. This consists of starting at one corner of the room and working to my right until I have thoroughly covered all four walls. I wipe down everything in my path with cleaning spray and a dust rag, including the walls. And just for kicks, I count strokes. Thirty, thirty-one, thirty-two, done…

I vacuum the furniture and then the floor, again counting the strokes across the fabric in each direction. I then decide to wipe down each mini blind covering the windows. Did you know that there are exactly ninety-six blades to each of my mini blinds? Yep, that's thirty-two if you divide by three, and there are three windows in each room of my apartment. That's 9 thirty-twos, which makes me wonder if I should change my derivative safe number to nine. But thirty-two divided by nine gives you 3.55555 to infinity. I like the repetitive fives, but have no idea how to apply that to my routine. You won't get an even number until you get to thirty-six. Thirty-six divided by nine is four. I could live with four.

But I think I'll just wait until my thirty-fifth birthday. Five divides into that evenly. But you get seven. There are seven days a week though. Seven could be so much fun. I wonder how old Edward is.

I spent five hours cleaning the entire apartment, and yes I planned it that way. I meticulously scrubbed every inch of the bathroom and kitchen. I even changed the sheets on the bed, even though I do that once a week anyway. I mopped the kitchen floor and took out all of the trash. Grabbing a soda from the fridge, I sat down on the sofa to admire my hard work. If Edward ever came over, he was sure to be impressed. I wonder if he might be at home this very minute doing the same thing to impress me. Did he have to? Did he want to?

Second thoughts interrupted my eagerness. I wanted to call Sallie and call all of this off, but I knew I couldn't. By now, she had rushed home and called Charlie to tell him the good news. Charlie had probably called Edward. A chain of events had been set in motion. I had just cleaned my apartment to make a good impression with someone.

It would be different if I met Edward in a chat room on the computer, and by him coming here it would be the very first time we ever met face to face. I somehow doubt that he'd come in and take one look at me and hate what he saw, but decide to spend the night because I keep a clean apartment. The apartment is part of the total package. I might even buy a new shirt or get a new haircut. I might buy some tanning sessions or some scented candles. For what? To make a good impression. And all for a date that we might hate anyway. All that time wasted, but we are more concerned about the chance that it won't be wasted.

In the bathroom that day, Sallie somehow morphed herself into someone presentable, someone who might make a good impression. She worked with what she had, and it worked out for her. Charlie was impressed. Had she not pulled her hair back that day or worn that red scarf, would Charlie never have called upon her again? I know those are material things, but they are part of the impression. What if Charlie hated red or if he preferred women with curly hair?

I take a newspaper from the end table and rip it in half. I scatter its pages across the armchair and let them spill onto the floor. I decide to leave them there for a few days, but I know I'll pick them up before Edward was to ever come over. My impression is not perfect though. I'm just me.

I look around the apartment and convince myself that my spring cleaning escapade was for me, all for myself, who I don't have to impress. There is one part of me in this apartment that I do need to change for Edward though. It's the pictures on the wall. Each collage of photos is all black and white, all framed in black with white mattes. They are all pictures that I took myself with my very own camera and had developed at the pharmacy photo counter. And they are all sad. If Edward ever comes here, he will wander from wall to wall to observe my hobby up close. There are no velvet ropes to keep both him and my art at a safe distance. And he will probably not like what he sees. He'll want to leave, no matter what the rest of the clean apartment looks like.

Twenty-Two

The method for steaming milk is a fine art form, all based on measurement and good timing. It also takes good equipment, which we definitely have at The Latte Da. The espresso machine and steamer costs over two thousands dollars alone. There is a mini fridge hidden under the counter directly under the espresso machine. It is set aside specifically for gallons of milk, of which we go through about eight to ten gallons on a busy day.

I am usually stationed at the espresso machine during the morning rush, and like everything else, I have my entire system all laid out to a series of strategic patterns based solely on the drink I'm making. It begins by hearing the customer order something such as a mocha or latte which will require milk. Based on the size they order and the quantity of drinks, I bend to the fridge and pull out one gallon of milk. I fill a metal measuring cup with the amount of milk needed and place the rest of the milk immediately back in the fridge.

Since most of the drinks ordered are hot, the milk will have to be steamed. There is a metal wand coming out of the espresso machine which I pull down into the measuring cup. I then pull a lever on the machine and a steamy screeching sound fills the air as hot steam is pumped into the milk. A thermometer clamped to the side of the measuring cup slowly rises and once it has reached a certain temperature I release the lever to stop the steaming process. If it is a drink that requires foam, while steaming the milk I slowly move the measuring cup up and down so that the wand spits across the surface of the milk, much like a child blowing bubbles in a soda with their straw. This movement creates sudsy bubbles of foam across the top of the milk which will be used when assembling the drink.

Espresso is the next ingredient, and the size of the drink the customer ordered determines how many shots of espresso will be used. While pouring the milk into my measuring cup, I push a button on the machine which grinds a certain amount of espresso beans to be used for about six shots. The grounds are dumped into a reserve located in the front of the machine. With the push of another button, I can tell the machine if I will need one shot or two. Grounds are then transferred into a tamper and packed down firmly while I'm steaming the milk.

When the milk is ready, I pour it into the specific size cup leaving about an inch of space from the top to allow room for the other ingredients. I use a spoon to hold back any foam because that will be put in last. The cup is then held under the pourer at the front of the espresso machine. With the push of yet another button, boiling hot water is poured through the tamper and the fresh espresso shots come trickling out of the pourer and into the milk. Depending on which button I pushed, one shot pours for a small drink and two shots pour for a medium or large.

I sit the drink on the counter and stir it with a long metal spoon to evenly blend the espresso and milk. If a customer ordered a latte with no foam, then my work is done. Sallie or Auden will take the drink from there, put a lid on it, and hand it to the paying customer. If a customer wanted foam, I scoop a few spoonfuls from my measuring cup onto the top of the drink and then I'm done. The customer pays three, four, or five dollars and that's a latte.

Anything else on the menu board requires a few extra steps, which if I'm not careful, can screw up my whole process. Unfortunately, dating is not as systematic. I can make a caramel macchiato or hazelnut latte in less than a minute and do it all while carrying on a conversation with Sallie and Auden at the same time. There is no spontaneity, which is almost required of dating otherwise someone would be bored. Sure, eventually the magic rubs off, your heart no longer skips a beat, the gifts for no particular occasion stop coming, and the two people go from dating to being boyfriends and girlfriends. It's the next step in the process.

There was a day when I knew nothing about pouring coffee or creating drinks, but I learned and now it's just second nature to me. I've been on dates before, but I still know nothing. No one really does. No matter how many times you've done it, each time is still a completely new and frightening experience and you are bound to make mistakes at it.

It's a task none of us will ever conquer.   I still obsess about it.

Twenty-Three

Despite asking Sallie to keep all of this double-dating business quiet, there is only one other person in both of our lives that either of us would tell. Auden. And although I probably would have told Auden about it anyway, Sallie beat me to it.

"So..."

"So?"

"I hear someone else around here has a date," Auden chimes.

"I have no idea what you are talking about. No further questions, please."

"Are you nervous?" Auden asks, ignoring my comedic tone.

"Not yet. I'll probably have a breakdown five minutes before I'm supposed to meet him."

"We all do that."

"We do?"

"Well, with blind dates why wouldn't someone be nervous?"

"So, you've been on a blind date before?" I ask.

"Many times."

"Did you ever cheat?"

"I'm not sure what you mean," Auden says, "How do you cheat on a blind date?"

"Well, did you ever spoil the element of surprise? Let's say a friend sets you up with another friend of theirs that you've never met, but maybe you know where they work or what class they are in at the art school. So, you go take a peek knowing that if they see you, they'll have no idea who you are anyway."

"Ahh, checking out your gifts before they get wrapped, huh?"

"Yeah, I guess you could call it that."

"Take a notebook," Auden says.

"What?"

"Take a notebook, and after you've seen that

unsuspecting person find a place to sit and write down everything about that first time you saw them, how you feel, what you think of them, all that stuff."

"Why would I want to do that?" I ask puzzled.

"Because, Blaine, if they are the one person that you end up spending the rest of your life with, some day you'll tell them about how you were there that day admiring them from across the room or in the hallway between classes. You can give them those thoughts you wrote down on paper. It'll make a nice gift."

"So, you always take a notebook?"

"I have. Once."

"Did you write something down?"

"I don't write. I paint or sketch."

"Did you ever give it to that person?"

"No. Not yet."

"Is it someone you are seeing now?"

"Yeah."

"Are you going to give it to them?"

"Maybe someday."

I take Auden's advice and pack a notebook with my camera. A few days later I decide to take a stroll through the University campus. The English building is located on the far corner of the campus flanked by parking lots on two sides and a nice open plaza on the other two sides. It's a tall narrow building with decorative molding around each window. Gargoyle faces are at the top of the building in each corner and above the doors. There's a bronze plaque on the side of the building dedicating it to some unknown doctor or professor, or someone who donated a lot of money to the department. I snap a picture of it. To passersby, this building is like any other on any campus across the country. There is nothing that makes it stand out from all the rest.

The plaza is a large open field framed by wide sidewalks on all four sides leading in between the other various surrounding buildings. Park benches line the sidewalks facing inward to the field of neatly trimmed grass. There is a concrete platform in the middle of the plaza probably used for gatherings, picnics, or speeches. The middle of the platform has been left open for an enormous oak tree that provides shade over the entire stage and the surrounding grass.

There is a large clock directly in line with the oak tree and the entrance to the English building. Its Roman numeral face sits on top of an ornate pole, and its body reminds me of an old grandfather clock with elaborate carvings. I take a seat on a bench on the opposite side of the plaza just to the right of the tree so that I have a clear view of everyone coming and going from the English building. I snap another picture of the tree, with the clock in the background and the door to the building behind it.

A pattern develops. I notice that the majority of students are casually dressed and are carrying backpacks. Professors wear suits or dresses and carry brief cases. Most of the professors look old enough to have personally known Shakespeare himself. In watching the clock, I notice that an influx of students arrives and crowds into the building about every twenty minutes, coming from all directions around the plaza and from the parking lot. No one walks directly across the grass in the plaza; they trek around it staying on the sidewalk. Then, it's as if the professors have to make the final entrance. Once the herd of students has gone inside, a group of two or three professors appear from across the campus and escort each other into the building.

I eventually spot Charlie approaching the building by himself. Like all of the other professors, he is wearing a dark suit. At first, I hold my notebook open across my face so that he won't recognize me. He appears deep in thought, perhaps thinking of Sallie. He never looks in my direction. I slowly reach for my camera from around my neck and hold it over the notebook. I zoom in and snap a picture of him just as he comes within view of the clock.

I may not record any thoughts on paper today to be able to give to anyone tomorrow, but I'll have a nice picture to give to Sallie on an anniversary, or maybe even a wedding day.

Twenty-Four

After an hour of sitting in the plaza and admiring the campus through the eye of my camera, I decide to go inside the English building. So far, I haven't overheard any conversation that suggested it could be Edward. I also haven't seen a professor that I hoped could be Edward. I knew I'd increase my chances by going inside, but I also feared running directly into him. What if I stopped to ask someone if they knew where his office was, and they turned out to be him? The anticipation was both nerve-wrecking and exciting. My heart raced as I climbed up the steps and opened the door. I liked the adrenaline rush and the blood pounding in my ears. I forgot how dating could be so much fun.

The main floor consisted of just a plain square corridor with an elevator on two sides opposite the door I had just entered. There were hallways down each side of the elevators that led to a few classrooms. Groupings of dusty and wilted potted plants stood in each corner surrounded by a few ottomans where some students were sitting and reading. On the wall opposite the entry was a series of bulletin boards. I walked over hoping there would be a directory. There was.

I learned that the building was divided by departments. The main floor where I now stood was for beginning and intermediate courses for first year students. There were courses entitled *Basic Grammar* and *English 101*. The second and third floors were divided up for English and American Literature. The fourth floor was for Creative Writing, Poetry, and Workshops; and the top floor was where the staff offices were located. I took the elevator to the fourth floor.

I watched the numbers overhead light up at each floor. There was a quaint *ding* announcing the arrival of the elevator on the fourth floor. Ding! The toast is ready! Ding! The microwave popcorn is done popping! Ding! Blaine had arrived to spy on his date! It made me laugh out loud. Thankfully, I was alone in the elevator. The doors slid open and I noticed there was

78

a wall opposite the elevator; I could only go left or right. I chose left and thought I would walk the entire hallway just to get acquainted.

I discovered there was just one square hallway that outlined the entire floor leading to the second elevator at the other end and eventually back to where I started. Classrooms lined the hallway down each side with only numbers on the doors. There were more ottomans up and down each side of the hallway, so I took a seat to think about what I should do next.

I got up to walk the hallway again and counted classroom doors, trying to look like a lost student. I thought someone might offer assistance and I could just ask them where the Poetry classes were taught, but all the classes were in session so no one else was in the hallway but me. The numbers on the doors started with a 4, obviously signifying that I was on the fourth floor. Would it just be coincidence if I told you that there were indeed thirty-two doors? This was meant to be.

I noticed the last door did not have a number on it. The numbers down the hallway stopped at 431. I was intrigued. I sat on an ottoman nearest this last unmarked door for at least fifteen to twenty minutes just knowing that Edward would soon emerge. Suddenly, the sound of cans crashing to the floor came from behind the door followed by giggling and someone shushing the laughter. My curiosity got the best of me, and I found myself reaching for the doorknob.

I turned it slowly and found it unlocked. As if in slow motion, I opened the door and light from the hallway began to fill the small room. It was a broom closet. An array of spray cans were scattered across the floor. Propped up on a trash can was a husky cleaning lady with smeared lipstick and her giant tits hanging out the front of her tank top. An elderly man, with skin like a raisin, in a janitor suit was holding her leg up in one hand and groping her breast with the other. They both froze and looked at me like owls in a barn.

"I guess this isn't 18th Century French Poetry?" I asked, trying not to humiliate them.

"Son, it could be," The old man exclaimed with a

toothless cackle.

I snapped their picture and quickly shut the door.

Twenty-Five

I was giving up. The broom closet was a sign. It's a straight man's world, and I'm just a jester in his court. I grabbed the next elevator and punched the button to the ground floor, convincing myself that coming here was a bad idea. Maybe even agreeing to the blind date was a bad idea.

Ding...

The elevator stopped for passengers at the third floor. Two students got on, a guy and a girl. The guy pushed the button for the second floor. The girl pushed the button for the ground floor, even though it was already lit. Why do people do that? Do they assume they need to let the elevator know that two people will now be getting off at the ground floor? The elevator will happily stay open long enough to let everyone get out. It's getting on that the elevator finds humorous, always closing its doors right at the last minute when someone is running for the door. The people inside are helpless and can't stop it. The door closes and the elevator lifts off, probably giggling to itself. The passenger left behind stands there in anguish pushing the button again and again to call the elevator back, but it won't come.

Neither passenger acknowledged me. The girl passenger is a pig-tailed short blond that probably waits tables at night. She's probably an English major with intentions to be a grade school teacher, or because she has no idea what she wants to be. Aren't those the two main reasons people major in English anyway? She probably *loves* kids and goes by her first name only like Candy, Christie, or Kathleen, "Hi I'm Kristy with a K, and I'll be your server tonight?" I can tell by her bubbly tone that she's actually a slut.

"Candy, I liked that last chapter. And hearing you read it out loud really gave it depth and perception," the guy said out loud.

"Thank you. I worked all night on it."

I bet she worked all night. On a downtown street corner.

"Do you have your three poems written for next week's

81

assignment?"

"I have two of them finished. Not quite done with the third, but I'll be ready," she says with batting eyes.

"Well, I'm looking forward to it."

"Thanks."

Ding...

We had arrived at the second floor. The elevator doors slid open and the guy paused as if expecting a hoard of people to trample him to get onto the elevator. No one was there.

"Enjoy the rest of your week, Candy. See you next week," he said touching her shoulder lightly and stepping off the elevator.

"You too, Professor," she said with a grin, even though the doors had closed and he was gone.

I rolled my eyes.

"He's so hot," she said to herself before turning to glance at the ghost over her shoulder.

I looked her way and gave a nod.

"Hi," she whispered.

"He *was* hot," I said blandly, "but he doesn't look like a professor."

"Who? Professor Edward?"

No, the other invisible professor standing next to me you dimwit! Who else? Edward? She said Edward.

"His last name is Edward?" I asked.

"I can't pronounce his last name and he gets mad when people say it wrong, so he has everyone call him by his first name. Edward."

I see "hot" people everyday in the park or in the coffee shop. Some days I see more than others, too many to even mention. The city is filled with hot people. You might say to yourself, "he's hot," and then never think twice about them. In Candy's case, she thinks out loud.

Professor Edward was indeed hot. I had failed to notice for longer than a few seconds, not thinking this could be my Edward. My eyes were still burning from what I saw in the broom closet. My mind was set on Edward, so other people around me were coming and going in my brain as quickly as they were in person or from the elevator. I had mistaken him for a student based on how he was dressed, so I had quickly dismissed him as a suspect.

"Isn't there another Edward who teaches poetry?" I asked. I wanted to be sure this was him.

"Nope. He's the only Edward in the department," Candy said rocking on her heels.

Ding...

The elevator had arrived at our destination on the ground. I stood against the back wall unaware of anything. I was trying to make a mental note of how Edward had looked. Auden was right. I needed to write it down. It had all happened so quickly. There was no time. If I didn't write it down now, I would forget.

"See ya," Candy said, knowing we'd probably never see each other again, but the word good-bye is complicated.

Luckily, no one was standing there behind the metal curtain as it slid away. I still had the elevator to myself and didn't look like an idiot to anyone for not stepping out. The doors slid closed and I expected the elevator to rise up again to pick up someone calling it on a floor overhead. It just sat there, like on a quick smoke break or something. I pushed the button to go to the second floor and just knew the elevator was cursing me.

Ding...

The doors slid open again. No one was standing there. I lifted my camera and took a picture from my viewpoint looking out of the elevator into the hallway leading to the rooms on the second floor. I waited. A few seconds passed and the doors glided shut. I snapped another picture just as they were closing, catching only a glimpse of what was behind the doors.

So Edward wasn't in the picture, but at least I had a picture of where I first saw him. It's a picture he wouldn't understand at first, but in time if he got to know me he'd get to know it too. The elevator was where our paths first crossed, unbeknownst to either one of us.

Ding...

Twenty-Six

Back outside in the plaza, I took a bench and began to write in the notebook everything I could remember. I'm amazed at how much my mind can recall as I write it all down, even though I only saw Edward for a few brief seconds.

Edward was wearing clean white sneakers, or maybe they were black. His khakis were slightly wrinkled but nice fitting and fraying on the ends. He was wearing a tight green polo tucked in, showing a plain brown belt around his tiny waist. He was lean but muscular. I remember the veins in his arms when he reached for the elevator button. His shirt hugged a flat stomach and slightly formed pecs. His shoulders were broad. His skin was a creamy tan. His hair was blondish brown and extremely curly, but it was cut very short so it appeared fuzzy.

Edward's eyes were a sky blue, or maybe they were cat-eye green. We didn't really make eye contact for me to know for sure, but they were like golf balls. Big round eyes. I do remember a spray of freckles across his nose and cheeks, probably from too much sun. His lips were probably inherited from his mother, very puffy as if swollen. Kissable. He hadn't shaven that morning so he was a bit scruffy, but his jaw line was smooth as if he didn't have to shave much at all. So, maybe he kept the scruff on a regular basis. Rugged. I liked it.

His voice was deep but not explicitly manly. He sounded like a professional public speaker, apparently well-spoken in front of a classroom. I imagined people wanted to listen to him and were mesmerized by the things he had to say. He cleared his throat a lot. Maybe he secretly smoked or Candy just made him nervous.

He was the epitome of the young former Rugby playing all-American teacher that both female students and colleagues whispered about. Candy was probably still fantasizing about Edward as she walked to her next class. The fact that he was single just increased the odds. He was available, so they didn't hate him. Women never really hate the man they dream about though; they hate is wife or girlfriend. So based on Candy's reaction, no one knew he was gay either.

I tried to picture us sitting next to each other across from Sallie and Charlie. I envisioned us holding hands while cuddling on the sofa on our first date by ourselves. I imagined us taking a walk in the park. Holidays together. Sex. Sleeping late on Sundays in a sweaty heap under the winter blankets. I tried hard to picture all of these things, but none of them seemed real. Based on what I wrote down, I wasn't even sure he was gay. Despite everything being so right about him, he had to be the wrong Edward.

Twenty-Seven

"Did you see him?" Auden asked the next day at work when he arrived at noon and Sallie had left for lunch with Charlie.

"I think I did."

"What do you mean?"

"Well, I saw an Edward; I'm just not sure if it was my Edward."

"Did you speak to him?"

"No."

"How do you know it was him? Had Sallie shown you a photo?"

"No. A student told me. They got on the elevator with me and were talking. She called him Edward, so I asked her about him when he got off the elevator."

"What did she say?"

"She said he was hot."

"Was he?" Auden asked.

"He was. Yeah, he definitely was."

"You don't sound convinced."

"I don't think he's my type."

"Not your type? Why not? You said he's hot."

"He is, but there's got to be more than that."

"He's smart. He teaches poetry. He's obviously creative. What more could you want?"

"I don't know what I want," I said.

"You want to get laid," Auden said.

Rather than it sounding like a question, Auden said that in a bit of a demanding voice as if he knew what I really wanted. At this point I really wasn't sure what I wanted, and I hate when other people think they do know what you want and sort of push their view upon you without really asking. Auden never asked me what I wanted. He just assumed I should be interested in Edward because he was attractive, creative, and might put out.

None of us are very sensitive when it comes to other

86

people's needs, just as Auden never took the time to really ask me what I expected from Edward. I have no idea what I would have answered with. I honestly have no idea what I really am expecting from all of this. The reason no one asks what we want is because no one really cares. We're all so absorbed in ourselves that we'd rather force our own opinions down each other's throats as if they were more important. We prefer to talk rather than listen.

Case in point, all of Auden's nighttime customers are from the art school. They all bring their unfinished canvases and projects in to show off to one another, claiming they seek out inspiration and constructive criticism from each other. They say they feed off the creative energy of one another, like some sick finger painting vampires. Someone always ends up being the center of attention standing in front of everyone in the room and holding up some unfinished oil painting or pencil sketch while everyone critiques.

The problem is they all try to speak over one another with a better idea, trying to impress everyone with their knowledge of the subject matter or some brush stroke they learned when they took that class the previous semester. They all disregard the actual artist's point of view and just end up filling the room with boundless chatter.

"You should paint a tree on the left."
"You should add more blue."
"Use heavier outlines thinned with water."
"Try some greenery."
"Make the fruit a little less yellow."

Nothing gets accomplished, and chances are the artist will ignore all of their outlooks and end up doing what he set out to do from the very beginning. And that's exactly what he should do. We should listen to our own hearts and minds because most of our friends give bad advice anyway. They tell us what we want to hear, without listening to what we have to say.

Maybe a part of me did want to get laid. Maybe a part of me was happy that Edward was creative. Maybe I just want to get through the date without Edward noticing me counting the number of steps it took to get from the car to the restaurant door and back. I want Edward to ask me out on a second date before I ask him about his favorite number. I want to kiss him. I want a new best friend. I want to fall in love, and know he loves me back. I want to take his picture, and maybe let him take mine. Yeah. That's what I want. It's what I wish for.

I think.

But it's probably not what I will get.

Wishes don't always come true.

Twenty-Eight

I am not the yearbook toting jock living in my glory days who pulls out a photo album every time I have company. Outside of Sallie, I can't remember the last time I had company over. With Sallie, I don't pull out the most recent photos every time she comes over. At any given time, there is an array of unframed photos lying on my dining or coffee table. Sallie will often pick up a stack and thumb through them like magazines in a waiting room, and politely tell me which ones she likes. She occasionally asks for a copy, of which I just let her take and keep that photo from the stack.

She tucks them in her purse and I might later see one of them in a frame on her mantel in her apartment. She wouldn't point it out to me, but it makes me proud to find it there. A true friend does things like that, showing you that they really do care about you. They care about the things you care about, and they don't have to point out their efforts for you to take notice. It comes naturally just as such things should in a friendship. It's like someone giving you a greeting card for no special reason, or showing up to watch you play in a ball game although you never invited them.

Until now, Auden has been a different kind of friend. I considered him as being just an acquaintance or a co-worker. We had never hung out with each other outside of work, and what I knew of him was only what had been explored in friendly conversation behind the counter. But that could all be lies for all I know. We are all different around people we don't really know outside of work. And because we are different, we don't often try to get to know those people any better beyond that work-related atmosphere.

I know that Auden likes art and is covered in fairy-tale tattoos. I know that he looks like he sings in a punk rocker band and uses automobile oil on his hair, but he doesn't. He knows I like to take photos and that I sleep with men. I know he seems pretty asexual to me, or maybe he will date men or women. And that's about all we really know of one another, if you can count not really knowing at all as actually knowing anything. But that is about to change when Auden hands me a piece of paper.

"Here," he says digging in his man purse, a large well-worn brown leather bag that he carries with him.

"What's this?"

"Read it."

He hands me a clipping of a newspaper ad announcing a local photography contest. It is sponsored by the photography department at the art college, and they are inviting people eighteen years of age or older to submit pictures on any subject matter along with a one dollar entry fee. Three winners will be chosen and honored with a 300, 200, or 100 dollar prize. All photo entries will be put on display for two nights at the art college for the public to come and view. All proceeds will be used for a scholarship to the college. The three winning photos will be put on permanent display for one year framed in the lobby of the photography department.

"Wow! Why are you giving me this?"

"I know photography is your hobby, so I thought you might like to submit something."

"But you've never seen any of my photos."

"Sure I have."

"Where?"

"Sallie showed me. She always keeps one of your photos in a frame in her apartment. She's got lots of others you took, a whole album."

"You've been to Sallie's apartment?" I ask.

"Of course. Haven't you?"

"Well, yeah, but I just thought—"

"You just thought that I left work and climbed back under a rock somewhere," Auden says with a laugh.

"No, not at all. Nothing like that. I...I...I know you like art. You like to paint. I know you have a degree."

"And you know I work here and pour coffee just like you do, and that's all you know. Big deal. Those are things any customer who comes in every day probably knows," Auden said shaking his head and walking away from me.

"You are right. I've never taken the chance to get to know you more."

"Whose fault is that?" Auden asks while wiping down the pastry case.

Silence. I walk away to tend to the espresso machine.

"You don't know that much about me either," I finally call out to him over my shoulder like a stubborn kid.

Auden slams the pastry case door and rushes over to me. He grabs me by the shoulder and twists me around to face him. He wraps the collar of my shirt tightly in both of his hands and pulls me close to his face.

"I know that every day your entire morning routine is timed using your alarm clock because you are obsessed with the number 32. Your whole life is practically based around that number. I know that you like to dance. You like to go to pubs with Sallie. You're jealous of Charlie because you and Sallie don't hang out anymore. You like to take photos. You go downtown to Bachardy Park almost every day and sit and take photos of people and pigeons. You frame pictures of people you don't know and you hang them on your walls. And outside of this coffee shop and your camera, there isn't much more to know. Should I continue?" Auden spits.

"How do you know all that?" I stutter, "Sallie told you?"

"I know how to listen, Blaine," Auden says, "I'm a good listener."

"Okay," I say, swallowing hard.

My heart is racing. My complexion is probably turning either deep red or ghost white. A cold sweat forms across my forehead. I've never seen Auden get angry before.

"It's just sometimes people don't know how to speak to me, so there's no one to listen to."

And with that he lets go of my collar. I catch my balance and steady myself against the espresso machine, a bit embarrassed, wishing I was somewhere else right now.

Auden just walks away.

Twenty-Nine

Coffee shops should be referred to as ice breakers. If I ever open up my own shop, I'd probably call it The Ice Breaker. Coffee shops are the place to mingle for the under aged teens who can't get into bars. And I bet more business transactions have taken place in a coffee house than on a golf course. Friendly first dates often begin or end in coffee houses, especially between two gay men meeting for the first time. People leave online chat rooms and come to coffeehouses, or thanks to wireless internet they visit chat rooms while inside coffeehouses.

"Hey, let's meet. I'm already here. Come on down and join me for a latte," someone types.

So, it seems only fitting that I'd return to The Latte Da just before closing. I snuck in while Auden was busy with customers. I waded through the college kids bouncing from table to table and sat down at an empty table near the back. With a view of the entire place right in front of me, I wish I had brought my camera so that I could take a picture of this caffeine party. Instead, I brought several photo albums with me. I sat them down on the table and began flipping through them, waiting for the shop to clear out and for Auden to start closing down.

"Have you taken Framing 202 yet? That Ms. Johnson is a bitch, isn't she?"

I look up from the albums to see a young wiry-haired androgynous kid standing over me wearing a vest covered in all different kinds of hat pins and political buttons. He's smiling at me, waiting for me to answer his question.

"I'm not a student," I say, closing the album and putting a firm hand on top of the stack so that he can't reach for them.

"What year did you graduate?" He asks with wide eyes.

"I didn't."

"You dropped out?"

"No! I've never attended the art school."

"Oh, why are you here then?"

"I like coffee."

"But you aren't drinking any."

"I haven't ordered yet."

"Oh, you better hurry then. They close in about ten minutes. You should get a caramel mocha. Auden makes the best."

"Thanks."

He (or she) stands there for a few seconds obviously at a loss for words and unaware that our conversation has ended. I look back down at the albums, hoping he will go away. He still just stands there, fingering the empty chair across from me as if he is contemplating sitting down. I raise my head slowly and try to instill a sense of anger in my eyes.

"Good-bye now," I say with a quick nod to send him on his way.

"Oh! Yeah. Bye now. Don't forget to try that mocha," he says backing away and finally turning from me to walk out.

The rest of the shop has already cleared out. Auden locks the front door behind the kid. I open another album and start thumbing through my pictures, waiting for him to notice me.

"I see you met Chris," he says from across the shop where he has started to wipe down the tables and straighten the chairs. He doesn't look in my direction.

"Is Chris a boy or a girl?" I ask.

"No one really knows."

I laugh, looking back down at the photos and waiting for him to finish closing down.

"What are you doing here?" Auden asks, walking toward me but remaining busy with the tables and chairs.

"Well, I thought that maybe when you finish closing down you could sit down and help me pick a photo for the contest. I brought some albums if you have time."

He stops cleaning, standing there at a distance, and finally looks right at me, studying his answer from deep somewhere inside his head.

"How about that caramel mocha while you wait?"

"Okay."

"I'm almost done closing. I shouldn't be long."

"Want me to help?"

"No, that's okay. I'll finish. I like doing it on my own."

"Sure."

I couldn't stand the thought of someone being angry with me. I'm sure there are people who can't stand me somewhere in the world, a guy I cut in front of at the bar or some customer I pissed off. Everyone has enemies. I just can't think of any; and having one person, who I see almost everyday in my life, be mad at me was tearing me up inside. I wanted to make amends with Auden, if needed, as quickly as possible.

The lights in the office and behind the front counter were dimmed, a sign that Auden had finished his nightly routine. He came to the table with two drinks in hand, and he had changed clothes. He was wearing jeans and a baggy sweatshirt. It was the first time I'd seen him in anything that wasn't black. He looked at me taking note of his attire.

"What? Do you think Prince Charming wore his armor all the time?"

"What is the obsession with fairy tales?" I ask.

"You don't want to know," he says, shying from the question.

"I asked, didn't I?"

The look on my face is serious.

"Okay, fair enough. Fairy tales are one thing that almost all of us share as kids, right? Chances are you know most of the stories that I do. You can look at my tattoos and name every character," Auden explains, lifting a sleeve of his sweatshirt to reveal an arm inked in the child-like narration I've seen before, both on his arm and in books. "The stories never change and neither does their interpretation practically. But we change."

"You can't change your tattoos though," I say.

"Exactly. Just like those stories, they will always stay the same. I can add to them but I can't take away."

"So for you the tattoos are a reminder of one thing that's constant in the world?"

"You could say that, and I really do think they are cool for lack of a better word," he says with a snicker.

"I like them too. They're different."

"Thanks," he says blushing. "So tell me something I don't know about you?"

"Me?"

"Sure. You started this reveal."

I tried hard to recall the words that Auden had shoved into my face earlier that day, the tabloid headlines divulging the minuscule details that make up my big fat boring life. I thought of a string of things he had left out or probably did not know, but could not think of something to tell him that might enthuse him with awe. My life was uninteresting. Unlike Auden, I had no tattoos to tell.

"Do you know that Mexican bar and pub not far from here?" I asked.

"Molly's La Covina?"

"That's the one. Did you know that Covina isn't even a Spanish word?"

"I always heard that it used to be *Cocina*, which means kitchen, but that the wind blew the second C sideways so now it looks like Covina and they just left it that way."

"Yep, that's what I heard too," I laughed.

"So, what about Molly's?"

"I go there on Mondays for two-for-one margaritas."

"I've heard they have a great happy hour, but I've never been."

"I've gone every Monday for years now."

"That's great. You must really like margaritas."

"That's not the only reason I go," I say.

"What else is there?" Auden asks scrunching his eyebrows, wondering where I'm going with this.

"You probably know it's a huge hang out for gays, right?"

"Isn't that why they nicknamed it Jolly's?"

"I haven't heard that before."

"Go ahead with your story. Don't let me interrupt you. You go there because it's a cool hang out for gay people," Auden says.

"Well, sort of. Years ago I walked in on two attractive

guys wrapped up in a very alluring situation in the bar's bathroom. I embarrassed them, of course, because they'd been caught. They zipped up and rushed out of the bar, and I don't think they've ever been back. It intrigued me that people took such a chance and did something like that in public. It turned me on. So, I kept going back hoping to catch someone again or even get wrapped up in something like that myself."

"You keep going back to happy hour in hopes of having a tryst in the public toilet?" Auden asks.

"Yeah, am I sick?"

"A little crazy, but I wouldn't call you sick," Auden says, "Has it ever happened?"

"Lots of times, but usually the guys won't do much in the stalls. They'd always want to go back to my place since I lived so close."

"Did you take them home?"

"Yeah. Quite a few times," I said.

"That's so dangerous, and yet exciting. I never pictured you doing something like that," Auden said shaking his head.

"Believe me, it's definitely an adrenaline rush. All the both of you really want to do is get off, but in the back of my mind I always worried I was taking home some psycho who would tie me to the bed and hack me to pieces. Are you disappointed in me?"

"No. Why would I be? That doesn't make you a bad person."

"Just curious. It hasn't happened in months though."

"You stopped going?"

"No, I still go, but it's like the magic wore off. When you turn 30, it's like there's a light bulb over your head that goes out. Men suddenly aren't interested in you anymore. You've had your time, and now you are left to just sit at the bar and drink and watch everyone else going home with each other."

"That happens to all of us. Time is marching on, right across our face I'm afraid," Auden said.

"So, that's when I started obsessing over everything else instead."

"Wait. You mean not hooking up with guys in the bathroom at Molly's made you obsessive compulsive?" Auden asked.

"I like to think so. You don't believe me, do you?"

"Blaine, if that's what you wish me to believe then I'll believe almost anything you want to tell me."

The truth was I think it was actually the sexual liaisons that made me obsessive compulsive, not them ending. Before going to Molly's on Mondays, I'd meticulously clean the apartment from top to bottom. I'd put fresh sheets on the bed. Even though it was always dark by the time I left the restaurant with someone, and the lights in my apartment remained off, I still needed the apartment to be clean to compensate for the dirty act I was committing.

Now everyone has little good luck charms or motions they go through so they don't jinx their favorite team, or so they win lots of money at the casino. My mother plays bingo with a woman who eats peanuts for luck. And so my own good-luck charm became the number on my apartment door. 32. Each night as I locked the front door and headed to Molly's, I would outline the numbers with my fingers, the three with my left hand and the two with my right. And it seemed every time I did it, I brought someone home that night. Just out of curiosity, I skipped doing the method one night and went to the bar, and went home alone that night.

But what if I moved and my apartment number changed? As a test, I locked my door one night and stepped over to apartment 33. I did the same routine outlining the numbers and then went to Molly's, and I also came home alone that night too. It was 32. 32 was my number. That was four years ago. Now I'm thirty-two years old, and by now the magic of the number seems to be rubbing off. I haven't taken anyone home from the bar in almost a year. So, instead I've applied the number to the rest of my life hoping for good fortune in other ways.

"Has it worked?" Auden asks.

"I don't really know. It controls my life, Auden. I feel like I have to go through these routines and patterns everyday, and for what? Just to get to work and sling coffee."

"Do you feel like something bad might happen if you don't do the routines?"

"I haven't really thought about it. It just becomes habit; I haven't really thought of the consequences of not performing them. I just do it," I said.

"Have you sought out professional help, maybe looked up medications?"

"No, you are the first person I've told about how this all began."

"You haven't even told Sallie? You mean she doesn't know about your one-night-stand addiction?"

"No."

"Why not? I thought you told her everything."

"Everything but this. Remember how Sallie acted when she first met Charlie? She kept him all to herself, like a new toy. You know everyone does that when they meet someone new, like they don't want the person to meet their friends just yet. They want them all to themselves."

"I think that is where your problem really started, Blaine."

"What do you mean?"

"You spend too much time alone. You crave companionship, even if it has to come from some anonymous guy you met in a public restroom. It's all you think about, and when you weren't getting it your mind tricked you into doing other things in order to think about something else. Think about it. We all want love, and most of us probably develop crazy habits out of time spent not being in love. Not making love."

"You really think that's it?" I ask.

"Just my opinion."

"I hope all that's about to change."

"We can only hope."

Thirty

With quite a bit of fascination, Auden sifted through my photo albums carefully studying some pictures and quickly turning past the others. He's the only one I could possibly think of to ask for help on picking a picture for the contest. He can appreciate the artistic value of my work. He gets me. By the time we finished with the albums, we had collected a pile of about twenty photos.

Together, we tried to imagine what lots of other people would probably be snapping photos of for the contest. There would be lots of flowers, zoo animals or wildlife, birthday parties and kids, landscapes and sunsets. In my own selection, there were only about three or four of foliage and one of a sunrise over the city. We removed those from the stack.

We also decided to rule out any architecture. People love to snap photos of the bridge over the koi pond at the Botanical Gardens or the neon sign atop the Peabody hotel downtown. We'd all seen those images before and although I had not taken photos of either of those elements of the city, I had plenty of others that we also put away.

That quickly narrowed our choices down to four photos. There was a snapshot I had taken of an old homeless man puking in an alleyway mid-afternoon down on Beale Street. He was bent over, steadying himself against the wall of a building, with drool streaming from his mouth like a cobweb. Auden appreciated the photo because he said it's rare for someone to catch something so unrehearsed. The picture was real. It was life on paper, both undisturbed and disheartening.

The second photo was of a live robin sitting on the shoulder of an angel statue in the Elmwood Cemetery. The angel's head was bowed in prayer, its hands clasped at its chest. Its wings were spread, tall and graceful. The bird's head was cocked to the side as if curiously wondering why the angel was not acknowledging it. This photo was quickly moved to the "No" pile because although Auden loved the infrequent moment I had captured, he knew there would be lots of other entries of angel statues in cemeteries. Like anything else in society, we all find beauty in similar things. We copy each other with our appreciation of what's around us. No one would have my photo of the robin, but the chance of someone else having a different depiction of the exact same angel was almost guaranteed.

That left two photos. One was of Charlie and the clock at the University plaza, and the other was of the little girl and the flying pigeons in Bachardy Park. Since Charlie and Sallie were still unaware I had even snapped that photo of him, Auden said I might want to put it on reserve. The contest was still several weeks away, so I had time to warm up to Charlie and show him the photo to get his approval. Auden loved the way Charlie was holding his hand to his chin while walking, so intent on getting where he was going, so deep in thought. I had not noticed a student in the background looking at his watch, even with the large clock lurking so near him. I guess in a way I was like that student, failing to observe the most obvious things around me.

But I had noticed the way Auden would hold one of my photos up to his face and scratch his chin, and then he'd glance over the top of the photo at my face as if he was comparing me to the photo. He'd quickly glance back at the photo when I would look up and make eye contact with him. There was a lot more than admiration there in his eyes. But I was doing the same, just doing a better job of not getting caught. When he would lean down over the table with the top of his head facing me, I'd lean forward to sniff his black spiked hair. It smelled fresh and soapy. I wanted to reach over and run my hand through his hair, but the spikes looked so pointy and hard. I imagined a wild animal discovering a porcupine in the forest with its hard quills aimed at him.

So, we both decided the snapshot of the little girl in the park would be the entry for now. It was an obvious choice for me, with it being so recent, but I was happy to see that Auden and I thought alike. I was glad to share so many of my photos with Auden and get his input. Auden nodded with approval, praising me for the photo. He said it gave him goose bumps. The little girl's innocence was so pure and natural. The blur of pigeons in flight and the tossed popcorn floating in freeze-frame around her were as if the mad spinning world had just stopped for a second. Just for her.

That night, sitting across from Auden, I think my world stopped for a second too. That look in his eyes was vague and blurred or maybe I just had a bad judge of demeanor. For now, my pigeon girl photo would do, but I had a feeling my true shining moment was still out of frame.

Thirty-One

Honestly, I still didn't know if Auden was gay or not. Or at least I didn't know for sure. As I said, I had never taken the time to get to know him any more outside of his appearance nor outside of work. And out of the very few things that I did know about him, his sexual preference was not one of them. Therefore, the chemistry I thought I felt between us over my photos at the coffee shop may not have been mutual.

But like any opportune moment that presents itself to us when we aren't paying attention, I never thought to approach him on the subject matter until we had turned out the lights to The Latte Da, locked up, and each gone our separate ways after saying good-night. I could ask him tomorrow at work, but would he ridicule me for having worked with him this long and not already known? Do I chance looking like I might be interested in going out with him? He'd be flattered but let me down by saying he liked girls this week. I would be forever humiliated. I'd have to quit my job, never to show my face in the coffee house again.

Sallie would call me ballsy just for asking him or scorn me for not already knowing Auden had a girlfriend. Did he have a girlfriend? Did he have a boyfriend? I can't recall ever hearing him discuss a night out with someone, a date, or a romantic road trip somewhere. Instead, I decided to leave this fine line between Auden and myself drawn on a chalkboard of intrigue and mystery, swept under the rug, come and gone from my mind as quickly as any other illogical thought. Could I be attracted to Auden? Could he be attracted to me?

For now, I would never find out. For now, I'd leave all the guesswork to Sallie, the matchmaker. Actually, there was no guess work. She was setting me up on this blind date with Edward and all I had to do was show up. Now that was easy. So for now, I put Auden out of my head. He was back to being a coworker and a friend, and the possibility of anything else escaped me. For now, my thoughts turned to Edward. A funny word: now.

Now isn't just now. It's a day later, or a day before, a year later than this time some time ago. It's labeled with an hour and a date, a week, a month, or a season, rendering all past *nows* antiquated or obsolete. But sooner or later, quite certainly it will come. Now.

And it had.

"So, how about this Friday night?" Sallie asked the next day at work.

"The double date?"

"Yeah, Charlie was thinking of having all of us over for a casual dinner. He might even grill out and then maybe we can play board games or something."

Board games? So that's what straight people do when they set up their gay friends on blind dates. How safe.

That was three days away. In just three days, I'd be stepping back onto the dating scene for the first time in months. Hell, make that a year. Sure, my experience was sketchy but there was no rule book to consult. How much could dating have changed over the past year, especially in the gay community where the word *dating* doesn't even exist in our vocabulary? Even thinking back, I can't remember when I ever actually went on a physical date with someone. I just met them at the bar, slept with them, and then left a spare toothbrush at their apartment. There was no "pick me up at seven, dinner out, split the bill, late night movie, kiss at the door, I'll call you" kind of date.

Still, I was nervous.

Who said, "Fear tweaks the vagus nerve?" I think it was Isherwood. He said, "fear is a sickish shrinking from what waits, somewhere out there, dead ahead."

The vagus nerve is the longest of the cranial nerves. Its name is derived from Latin meaning "wandering". True to its name the vagus nerve wanders from the brain stem through organs in the neck, thorax and abdomen. Had I too been wandering down a spaghetti-like winding trail made up of arteries and veins pumping nowhere, in search of companionship in all the wrong places, in all the wrong faces? Could Edward be the means of my journey, just a heartbeat away from the breath of life my social existence was in need of? I know, I know. I'm obsessing over it.

I also know the anticipation will kill me over these next three days, waiting.

Wishing.

Thirty-Two

Bombs fell, shattering the walls of Berlin in late 1940. The damage was slight, but the innards of buildings were exposed as brick and mortar crumbled into the streets. The coppery scent of gunpowder lingered in the air, which was a hazy film of soot and dust. The streets were littered with burning paper and rubble. Gunfire echoed in the distance. Candles burned behind shattered windows where families prayed over dinner, showing no signs of wanting to evacuate.

In the heart of the capitol of Nazi Germany, people darted through the streets before sundown, stepping over piles of bricks and debris to get inside a club. A hole in the wall, where a door and a window had once been, now exposed the inside of the club where a row of people both sat and stood all along the bar. They drank and laughed as if the cave-like opening behind them was nothing different. The onset of war had only changed the surroundings; it had yet to change the people.

Isherwood wrote quite a bit about this war-torn Germany, visiting Berlin just after these weak bombings had taken place. He made note of the barhops and revelers that still cherished every last minute they had left to celebrate in this city they loved, celebrating life before the arrival of Nazi soldiers who would force them out or arrest them, or shoot them. There was no bit of hesitancy to prepare for the onset of this hostile storm.

Just as in Isherwood's writings, a battle was brewing in my brain all leading up to Friday night when I would be introduced to Edward, but there was nothing I could do to stop it. Anxiety was in control as I pondered what to wear or tried to write a top ten list of good conversation topics.

"Don't worry. Edward is a lot of fun," Sallie assured me.

How "fun" should someone be over a dinner date? It wasn't like going to an amusement park with someone, or was it? Sallie had already met Edward over dinner at Charlie's. She knew what to expect. Would Edward eventually wind up drunk and stand up in front of everyone telling bad jokes? Would he force everyone into a game of strip poker and then cheat?

Sallie had the privilege of having already met Charlie face to face and gotten to know him. She had a head start on him as an acquaintance. Unlike her and Charlie, I'd never have the chance to meet Edward for the first time, alone, and have him all to my stingy self for a few weeks, relishing our time together and choosing not to introduce him to my friends just yet. I'd never have that giddy feeling like a kid with a newfound pet at home in a shoebox.

Friday night arrived all too quickly. I was both thankful and in shock at how quickly the days rolled by. I had x'ed off the blocks on the calendar like a pregnant woman counting down trimesters. I had changed my choice of wardrobe at least twice each day. Sallie knocked at my door on time, as usual, to pick me up and drive to Charlie's.

I don't drive. I can't. Counting my steps and memorizing cracks in the sidewalk is quite alarming enough. Having to control a moving vehicle, and stay alert of other vehicles around me, while getting from point A to point B is much more difficult. I barely trust cars to stop now while I'm crossing the street. How could I ever trust them to stop on red when my light is green? I'd have to wait patiently for their car to come to a complete stop, and then wait a while longer just in case they were teasing me. All the while, cars behind me would start honking and yelling because I was causing them to lose their chance and getting to go. The light would turn yellow, and then I'd just give up and wait for the next one, causing traffic to pile up behind me. Who needs that stress? That's why I walk, or get Sallie to take me.

"You aren't wearing that, are you?" She immediately asked at the door.

"What's wrong with it?" I asked looking down and surveying what I thought was my final selection.

I had chosen a crisp white and yellow striped polo tucked into a freshly starched pair of khakis, a brown leather belt, and matching brown loafers freshly polished and with brand new shoe strings.

"You haven't worn that shirt since the last time you had a

date. Fashion has changed quite a bit since then." She pushed me aside and hurried into my apartment.

At my closet door, she madly thumbed through hangers of clothes like Mommy Dearest searching for wire hangers. She picked out a pair of faded well-worn jeans, a green summer tee, and pair of blue and white sneakers.

"Well, are you just going to stand there? Get dressed," she demanded.

I flipped the shoes off and scurried out of the khakis. I pulled the polo and my undershirt off, tossed them on the bed, and stood there in front of her in nothing but black socks and my new black Calvin Klein briefs. Sallie stood there for a moment, oddly admiring my physique.

"Nice underwear. At least you got something right."

"Thanks," I said, "So help me. Please."

"Change those socks to white and put on these jeans. Put the green tee on and tuck it in. No belt. Then, put that polo back on, and wear these sneakers instead. I'll wait in the living room. Hurry."

She closed the door and left me to the heap of clothes on my bed. I recalled each step she had given me in my head verbatim. I emerged from the bedroom feeling like a model working the runway as I walked through the living room. Sallie sat deep in thought studying me.

"Untuck that polo," she said.

"But—"

"Do it!"

"If you insist," I said pulling the end of the polo from my jeans.

Sallie marched over and retucked just the front part of the polo into my waistline.

"Should I pull the jeans down to my knees and add a few gold chains?" I asked.

"Smart ass. Lots of guys are tucking their shirts in like this these days."

"Lots of guys half my age," I said rolling my eyes.

I looked at her attire and tried so hard to find something to pick at. There was nothing. She had somehow become a smart dresser since she had become un-single. She was wearing tight jeans with some sort of glitzy glittery curl on the back pocket, and a shiny Hello Kitty blouse. It was really a tee shirt, but if a woman tucked her tee in it magically turned into a blouse. Her hair was down, over her shoulders, and curly. Her make-up was immaculate, if she was even wearing make-up at all. It looked so natural it was hard to tell.

"Are we ready?" she asked.

"Sure," I said with a huge exhale.

"You'll be fine," she said patting my back. "Don't worry. Edward is very nice and according to Charlie he's excited about meeting you. Charlie is looking forward to spending time with you as well, if that means anything to you."

"I've never had a forgy. Oh wait, will you even be participating?"

"Shut up," Sallie said slapping me on the back.

We laughed.

I needed to laugh. I needed to hear her laugh. It felt like old times again, like couples night out and maybe we were headed to a movie or a bar. Just Sallie and me. I'm glad we were at least doing this together.

The gunfire in my head subsided.

Thirty-Three

Charlie lived in a quaint cottage style home very close to the University. His house was in one of those typical subdivisions where all the homes look the same. The yards are immaculately kept with a single tall tree in the front yard and perennial bushes in the flower beds, all perfectly trimmed and neat. Flagstone pathways lead from the heated driveways, where an expensive car sits to compete with the neighbors, to the front door which is red or mahogany.

No one goes through the front door though because that just leads to a cold and fancy sitting room where no one ever sits. That part of the house is like the fine China mothers only use for holidays and special occasions, and even then if it's just family she pulls out the paper plates instead. In Charlie's case, his sitting room was adorned with trophies, framed awards and plaques, and family pictures. Like most family homes, it was a sort of walk-in photo album silently screaming, "Look what I've done." All that stuff was from his past though, although proudly on display. He presently "lived" in the rest of the house, which is why we used the back entrance.

I point this out because I've always been intrigued by how social status somehow determines how many entrances we can have to where we live, no matter how ridiculous that may sound. Think about it. I work in a coffee shop just a few blocks from where I live. I enter through my front door, my only door, into my living room where I actually spend quite a bit of time living.

Charlie lives in an expensive tract house that looks just like his neighbors, also just a few blocks from where he works. And yet the front door of his house leads to a museum of his life, a room where he doesn't live at all, and entry from the outside is forbidden. The room is probably very much like a museum, cold and dark and you aren't allowed to touch anything. I abhor people who buy large houses because they feel like they need so much space and devote an entire room to celebrating their accomplishments, put it at the very front of the house, and then forbid you to walk through it. I started walking up the flagstone to that door just as Sallie shunned me.

"Charlie never uses that door. It leads to his sitting room," she says.

I stop and turn around to follow her to the more appropriate side door, but not before I spy about a week's worth of newspapers sitting in front of the front door, next to a stack of three or four phonebooks inside wrinkled mud-caked plastic bags. How are unsuspecting paperboys and phonebook delivery boys supposed to know you don't use your front door? What if the UPS man brought a package for you when you weren't home and it was a very important package that you didn't even know was coming? Maybe it's the ashes of some long lost dead relative who left you as a contact and they arrived to you in a box full of money from their entire life savings. What if the UPS man left the package at your front door that you never use?

Yes, I'm obsessing over something so trite. I'll stop. I'm just nervous.

But if Charlie ever visits my apartment, I think I'll make him come in through the window.

Thirty-Four

Sallie took my hand in hers like it was my first day at kindergarten. She led me past the convertible in the driveway, which I assumed was Edward's. Charlie's car was probably in the garage. We crept around the garage headed toward the backyard, down a shimmery wet path of deep pea gravel. My balance tugged at Sallie's arm as if I was sinking into quick sand. She gave a glance at me over her shoulder as if I was turning to run. I wanted to. Instead, I raised my eyebrows and grinned. I exhaled a deep breath I had been holding, like a pop singer waiting in the wings to go on stage in front of millions.

The scrunching sound of our shoes sinking in the gravel gave us away. A beautiful pergola covered deck revealed itself as we turned the corner to the back of the house. Charlie, with spatula in hand, was tending to a large propane grill that was bigger than my apartment stove. He was already looking in our direction with a wide smile frozen on his face. He reminded me of an overanxious pet dog hearing their owner walking in the front door after being gone all day, at attention and ready to run and pounce.

"There they are. Hey guys!" Charlie yelled.

And then there he was.

Edward had been sitting in a deck chair. He quickly stood, with an iced drink in one hand, wiping his other hand across his shorts to rid his palm of either sweat or condensation from the sides of his glass. His cheeks blushed red when he stood, and then faded like a dying candle. He swallowed hard and looked swiftly in my direction but avoided my eyes. Surprisingly, I felt composed, having already been through several stages of apprehension these past few days. I was relieved to find Edward just now experiencing that rush of blood to the head.

Sallie released my hand as we climbed the five stairs of the deck. She stood on her tip toes to give Charlie a peck on the lips. He reached to shake my hand with that firm shake I remember from the first day I met him.

"And this is Edward. Edward? Blaine," Sallie said. She stepped aside with a flourish of the hands like a game show model revealing my door number one prize.

His smile widened to reveal teeth and he extended his dry hand to shake mine. His was also a firm shake. I squeezed back.

"It's very nice to meet you," Edward said.

"You too."

I suddenly remembered his deep voice from the elevator at the University, and his eyes were green, not blue. I got lost in them for a few seconds, and wasn't for sure how long I might have stood there with his hand still gripped in mine with neither of us saying anything. He had not shaved today either. I wanted to reach over and brush the back of my hand against his jaw, feeling the bristle of his five o'clock shadow. There was something he wanted to do too. I could see it in his eyes. Run and hide, maybe? No. It was much more magical. *Do it. Touch me,* I thought to myself, trying to will it (wish it) to happen. Instead, at the same time, we broke away from the hand shake.

"So, you work with Sallie?" he asked. He sat back down in his deck chair and offered the one next to him to me.

This was the part of the soap opera where Charlie and Sallie hovered together at the grill coddling over one another with an occasional giggle in the background. The camera would trade shots between myself and Edward as the conversation played out.

"Yes, we work together at her coffee shop."

"What's it called?"

"The Latte Da."

"Interesting name."

"It's supposed to sound like la-dee-da. We joke sometimes that she should open another coffee house or a sub shop and call it The Whoop-Tee-Do."

He laughed a sincere booming laugh. It was the kind of laugh that carried over a crowd in a bar or that you could hear from another room. It was a pleasant laugh that made you smile. It was contagious. And then we were silent for a beat, watching Charlie nonchalantly squeeze Sallie on the buttocks while she played out daddy's girl curious over how to grill burgers.

"She's the best thing that ever happened to him," Edward said to me a bit under his breath.

"He's the only thing that's happened to her."

"Really?"

"Well, since I've known her. Neither of us has dated much these past few years, nothing serious anyway."

"Really?"

"Yeah. What about you?"

"I was in a four year relationship. It ended a while ago."

"I'm sorry."

"Thanks, but there's no need to be sorry. Things happen."

We'd just met and I felt that he was already establishing which of us had more experience when it came to relationships. Four years is like an eternity among gay men so he definitely had bragging rights. It was the last thing he said that worried me. Things happen. What kind of things? He would probably avoid the conflicts with his ex in our conversation tonight, but was that his way of dismissing the subject? Maybe he was at fault for the relationship ending. Maybe he's difficult to get along with. Maybe he's a crazed butcher knife wielding psycho when he gets in an argument, and he killed his ex accidentally one night when they got into a fight over what was for dinner!

Things happen.

"So, tell me what it's like working as a coffee barista," he said.

"You really want to know?"

"Sure. I've never done anything but teach. It's fun listening to someone else's employment woes for a change. Don't get me wrong. I love what I do, but right now I'd rather hear you divulge your secrets about what's in a latte. Charlie tells me you guys make the best."

"They're not bad," I said, "but there's no smoke and mirrors. It's just espresso and milk."

I continued by telling him all about my theory of how our coffee preference illustrates our social class. I always thought that opinion sounded smart, but also humorous. And indeed, it made him laugh. It made me laugh. It felt good to be telling it out loud to someone. To someone who wanted to listen.

Thirty-Five

Charlie was a superb cook. Dinner consisted of large juicy burgers with all the fixings, home style French fries, a fresh salad, and homemade sweet tea. We ate in the yard at a picnic table, Charlie and Sallie sitting side by side across from Edward and me. Conversation consisted of Charlie and Edward sharing their strange yet humorous classroom stories, while Sallie and I offered up retail horror stories and our favorite bitchy customers. Charlie's backyard was filled with our laughter as the lingering smoke from the grill drifted into the trees. Crickets sang overhead.

At some point, Edward slipped a hand over my thigh and rested it just above my knee. I turned my head to glance in his direction, acknowledging his hand there, but not moving it. Charlie and Sallie got up to clear the table and went inside to the kitchen to serve up ice cream for dessert. This was the part in the soap opera where scooping four bowls of ice cream would take forever or they'd pause for a quick make-out session against the kitchen cabinets, leaving Edward and myself to chat at the picnic table.

"This has been really nice," Edward said when they'd left.

"It has. It's been a long time since I've done anything like this."

"Oh?"

"Yeah. Friends. Food. Laughing. Sallie and I always spent a lot of time together before she met Charlie, but nothing like this. Just us two. I don't really have a lot of other friends. I don't know a lot of people," I staggered.

"Well, now you know me," Edward said. I was glad he had interrupted. It was as if he knew I was slowly coming to a loss for words and might end up saying something silly that I'd later regret.

"That's right. We'll all have to get together again soon."

"How about tomorrow night?"

"Should we ask Charlie and Sallie if they have anything

planned?"

"No. I was thinking more along the lines of just you and me."

"Just us?"

"Yeah," Edward said through a nervous laugh. His cheeks were slowly turning red again.

"Okay," I said, "any idea what you'd like to do?"

"Let's just play it by ear. Something spontaneous. Spur of the moment. Be thinking about what you'd like to do."

"That sounds great."

"Good."

Silence again. What comes next? We'd just made a date. Until tomorrow, what else was there to do?

"You've got a little bit of mustard there," I said pointing to the edge of his mouth.

"Oh? Where?" Edward licked the edge of his lips with his tongue at an attempt to wipe away the spice, reaching for a napkin just in case.

"Right there," I said, pointing to the spot on my own face.

"Can you...help me?" Edward asked handing me the napkin.

I took it from him and dabbed at his lips. He looked contently at my face, deep into my eyes, and then stuck out his tongue again to lick my hand teasingly. I jerked my hand away in surprise.

"Oh, sorry. Just playing," he said with a laugh.

I began to laugh too.

He took the napkin from my hand and threw it on the table. Still holding my hand, he placed it in his lap and put his hand back on my knee.

"I hope you don't mind," he said.

"Not at all. I told you this is nice."

"Did you get the mustard?"

I looked at his face, like a concerned mother about to spit-wash her son's face on the way to church, and admired his large puffy lips.

"There's still just a little right in the corner." I pointed daintily, avoiding the attack of his tongue again.

"I think this might help."

And with that he leaned into me and pressed his lips to mine. They were so moist, and the slight taste of mustard mingled well with the sweet musky smell of his face. I kissed back, squeezing his knee. He rubbed his hand idly up my thigh and rested it gently on my waist.

For the first time in years, my mind was blank. I thought of nothing, not even of Sallie and Charlie probably gawking at us from the kitchen window. I was in this moment with content and happiness. I didn't even count the seconds to mentally record how long the kiss lasted. Some kind of wish had finally come true.

Like dripping wax pouring over the very candlestick it came from, I was overcome with warmth and tenderness. It was as if Edward's affection was being breathed into my very mouth, cleansing me of the tough skin and bitterness built up over time, chipping away at the hard heartless shell that had long embodied the single me. When our lips would finally part, I'd be a new man. Emerged fresh from a baptism in a Southern church pond, or like a diver breaking the surface of the water as he comes up for air, the heart beat thumping in my ears would subside. I would breathe the breath of life of a not-so-single man. Not so single anymore. Not lonely.

My *now* had indubitably arrived.

Thirty-Six

My routine with the alarm clock came naturally the next morning, like an orchestra and a metronome. It would take more than a man kiss to cure my mental illness. However, I was still giddy from the night before. I styled my hair with gel and sprayed some cologne. Like Sallie with her wine and lingerie, I was probably giving the impression that I had sex with Edward but Sallie knew that was not true. She drove me home last night.

I know it sounds cliché, but that first kiss sure seemed like it lasted forever even though it was not the only kiss of the night. With perfect timing, Sallie and Charlie came back out with the ice cream just a few seconds after Edward's lips broke away. I looked away to avoid eye contact like a kid caught in the act, scratching the back of my head. Edward was blushing a bit again. Sallie just grinned and handed us our ice cream. She knew what had happened, even if she didn't watch from the kitchen window, but she remained quiet. Charlie was clueless.

After dessert, it was Charlie's idea to go for a walk. There was a park just at the end of his street with a nice brick paved trail through a grove of trees. It led to a clearing over a lake that was the perfect spot to watch the sunset. On the sidewalk out front, Charlie and Sallie walked hand in hand just a few feet in front of us. Both Edward and I walked side by side with our hands in our pockets.

Men who love men don't always have the luxury of public affection. I'm sure there are quaint little "gay neighborhoods" in cities like Chicago or New York where it is not uncommon to see two men or two women holding hands on the street every day. Homos in this city aren't as fortunate. We have one day of the year when it feels safe to hold hands on the street without being pummeled with rocks or even shot. That was Gay Pride Day in June. Hand holding was practically a requirement then, a slap in the face for the moral majority that ruled the other 364 days a year. I think closeted couples even came out just to hold hands and march on that day because the streets were always full of people I never saw out anywhere else at bars or at the coffeehouse. I wondered if Edward had ever gone to Gay Pride.

In the park, we stood as four and watched the sun sink across the grey sky. A goose and her goslings dipped across a shimmering mirror of fading orange, finding refuge in some tall grass on the shore of the lake. Sallie tickled Charlie's sides and ran, forcing him to chase her back down the path. She always knew the perfect moment when some alone time would be essential.

Edward and I turned and laughed, watching them disappear among the foliage. Then, he looked at me and smiled. I pretended not to feel the weight of his stare, still looking into the trees although we could not hear Charlie and Sallie's laughter now much less see them. Edward reached for my hand, taking it into his and giving it a squeeze. I squeezed back. Our eyes peered across the water, searching for the sun that was long out of sight.

"So this is what it must feel like to be them," Edward said.

"It's better than that," I said.

My other hand was digging in my pocket, hoping to find two coins for wishing. My pocket was empty, but it didn't matter. Tonight had already been so perfect. I had no idea what else I'd wish for.

At work, Sallie told me how she had let Charlie catch her among the trees and they made out briefly while lying on the ground. They remained clothed, but kissed and groped passionately while Edward and I stood by the lake.

"Do you like him?" she asked.

"A lot."

"He likes you too."

"How do you know?"

"He told Charlie."

"We're getting together tonight," I said.

"Really? You didn't tell me that."

"It was his idea."

"Where are you guys going?"

"I don't know yet. We didn't make definite plans or

anything. We're just getting together," I said.

The morning rush had died off early. Sallie was waiting for Auden to arrive so she could go to lunch. Our prep work for the lunch crowd was already done. I was stocking the condiment counter when the bell rang and I expected it to be Auden coming in. I didn't turn to look.

"Can't a guy get some service around here?" I heard a voice call out. It startled me. I turned quickly to apologize to the customer, and then noticed Edward was standing at the counter. "Just kidding," he said.

"Hey! How are you?" I ducked behind the counter and gave my hands a quick wash. "What are you doing here?"

"I just stopped in to make sure we are still on for tonight."

"Absolutely."

"Would you like for me to pick you up from here or do you need to go home first?"

"Here is good, if you are sure you don't mind."

"No. Not at all. Class is done for the rest of the day, so I'm free. What time do you get off from work?"

"Hi Edward," Sallie said appearing from the stockroom.

"Hi Sallie."

"I clock out at five," I said.

"You can leave early if you'd like," Sallie said to me.

"Are you sure?" I asked.

"Sure."

"How about four?" I said to Edward.

"Sounds great."

"Make it three," Sallie said. "Go have some fun. You deserve it."

"Alright, three it is then," I said. "Thanks Sallie."

"How about a latte while you are here?" I asked Edward.

"Okay."

Edward pushed a five dollar bill across the counter to Sallie while I was making his beverage. She pushed it back over to him and told him the drink was on the house. I put the lid on his latte and brought it to the counter to him. He picked it up and laid a greeting card on the counter in front of me. It had my name on it.

"I'll see you at three," he said, taking a sip of his latte and turning to walk out the door before I had a chance to inquire about the card.

I discretely tucked the envelope into my apron, hoping Sallie had not noticed it. No matter what it said, no matter what I hoped it said, I at least wanted that all to myself. I cannot remember a time anyone ever gave me anything for no specific reason. There was always a birthday or Christmas accompanied by greeting cards and gifts. I liked the feeling of someone thinking of me for no apparent reason, taking time out of their day to go into a store and pick out a card for me. Just for me. No birthday. No holiday. Just because.

Auden came in for his shift, anxious to hear all about how the double date went. I promised to tell him all about it after lunch. Sallie and I went to lunch together at the deli to gossip about our new beaus. The cute sandwich makers behind the counter didn't even get a second look from me today. My mind was completely set on Edward, so it was as if no other man in sight mattered. I didn't tell Sallie about the card he had given me. I had gone to the restroom before we left for lunch, and opened the card in there while I was alone. And even now, I'm not going to say what it said. I want that all to myself just a while longer.

Thirty-Seven

Do you know the feeling of accidentally breaking a mirror and cursing yourself over the mess as tinkles of glass fall to the floor around you? You almost lose your balance as you dance over the wrecked disco ball at your feet, trying to avoid the derelict pieces as you go to get a broom. You sweep the glass up, hoping it is good enough, as if there are invisible shards out of plain sight (and there usually is). Maybe you even pierce a finger on a sliver of glass. You pull back your hand as if you've touched a cactus. You inspect the finger for any sharp protrusion and find only a single drop of blood. You pop the finger into your mouth to suck out the pain.

Pieces of the mirror in the dustpan still reflect your image, but the whole picture is broken. And just as you dump the shards, that urban legend of seven years bad luck for breaking a mirror pops into your head and you can't help but wonder what destiny lies ahead. You'll forget about it the next day, but as this is happening it almost makes you sick.

Telling Auden about meeting Edward was a lot like that. I wanted to tell him just for the sake of someone wanting to hear it. I wanted to feel like a proud storyteller, only I mistook the aching inside as yearning pains of love, of feelings anxious to spend time with Edward again later this afternoon as I stood there talking about him. And maybe they were just those sorts of cravings, but something felt different about them. It's like when you are bragging about something, and you know you are bragging and shouldn't be but you go ahead and say what you have to say anyway. It was as if I knew Auden didn't really want to hear me talk about Edward. He was only asking to be nice.

Auden listened contently. There was no sign of jealousy on his face, not even a sign of happiness for me. When I had finished, he only said one thing.

"That sounds nice."

Now maybe he was just having a bad day. A flood of customers did come in just as I had wrapped up my story. Auden immediately perked up and went into friendly customer service mode. But I couldn't help but think that maybe, just maybe, Auden was sad. He wasn't envious because I had met someone. He wasn't jealous because it sounded like this was going to continue for a while between myself and Edward. It was resentfulness. I couldn't help but think that maybe Auden was sad because he had let me get away.

No wonder men like fishing so much. When it comes to dating and fishing, they usually have a tall tale for both about the one who got away. Now I know nothing about fishing, and my dating skills are indeed rusty, but was I destined to become Auden's story of the one he regretted getting away?

It was approaching three and Sallie came out to relieve me so I could freshen up in the restroom if I wanted. I locked the door and took off my apron and read Edward's card again. I smiled and then looked firmly at myself in the mirror above the sink. There were no cracks in the mirror, only a small fracture in what I saw looking back at me.

Thirty-Eight

In 1967, Isherwood wrote a short book called *A Meeting by the River*. It's the story of two brothers, Patrick and Oliver, who meet in India after a lengthy separation. Oliver is the younger brother, very idealistic. He is preparing to take his last vows as a Hindu monk. Patrick is a thriving business man, a publisher who has a wife and children in London. He also harbors a secret. He has a male lover in the states in California. He publicly admires his brother's convictions, but privately criticizes Oliver's choices. Although this book is more about sibling rivalry and the competitiveness that can derive from those relationships, I think now of the secret Patrick was keeping from his family.

He loved his wife and children and the support they symbolically gave to his successful business life. What man doesn't want the breadwinner chevron on his jacket, proving how well he can financially care for the Misses and kids at home in the six bedroom mansion? But his heart wasn't there. His heart belonged to a strapping young man who dreamed of him every night in America.

As I stand outside the coffee shop waiting for Edward to pick me up, I peer back inside through the front glass, window-shopping the scenery inside. Auden and Sallie are busy with customers, each with beaming smiles of five star service that whisper "fuck you" under their breath to needy customers. I don't remember ever standing here on the outside, the business inside set to a different soundtrack of traffic speeding by on the street behind me. There is no hiss of the coffee maker, no bubbly gurgle of milk being steamed, no up sells of syrup shots, no "thank you come again." I am Patrick in London and this is my family. And I can't help but wonder if there on the inside of The Latte Da, there is a space in Auden's head, in his heart, dreaming of me.

Thirty-Nine

"Do you like the river?" Edward asks me in the car.

Isn't it odd that I was just thinking of that Isherwood book just before Edward picked me up, and these are the first words out of his mouth? The universe has an odd way of playing tricks on us like that. Some call it fate, some call it coincidence, but either way it's a wake up call, like gears inside a clock that all work in unison perfectly to keep the day moving, reminding us we are all connected.

By river, Edward means the mighty Mississippi that rolls lazily by the downtown skyline. I catch a glimpse of it between the buildings every time I go downtown to Bachardy Park, like an old friend you spot across a crowded room as they teeter between shifting people. It had been years since I walked along the river having photographed it long ago, but it too had become a tired postcard on the tourist rack in every gift shop or gas station. And so to me, it had become nothing more than a landmark, something pretty to look at but a part of the city I'd seen before.

Now it would be hard for a river to disappear overnight and no one notice immediately, but we sometimes take those things for granted. There was an old maple tree outside my apartment that I passed by everyday to and from work. Then one day, out of nowhere, I noticed the tree was completely gone and a flower bed had been put in its place. How long had it been since the tree went away? I tried to think of the last time I had seen it, but just assumed it had been there the day before and the day before that. My mind had somehow painted the tree's psychic energy right there in its place permanently, so even if the tree had been gone a month my eyes still saw it there and paid no attention to any changes.

Upon asking around, I learned that over a week before a garbage truck had swerved to miss a dog and run up over the sidewalk, hitting the tree while I was away at work. The tree had come crashing down, but kept the truck from running directly into the apartment building. I couldn't believe that tree had been gone for over a week before I had even noticed. It saddened me. It was like learning that an old friend you haven't seen in years had passed away. You get lost in thought trying to remember the very last time you saw them. So like visiting an old friend, I was happy that Edward suggested we take a walk along the river.

"I hope my card didn't frighten you," Edward said with hesitation.

"No, not at all. Thank you. It was a pleasant surprise."

"I love doing those sorts of things, just trying to make someone feel special and let them know I was thinking of them."

"I really appreciate it. No one has ever done anything like that for me before."

"Really?"

"Never."

My toes had just touched the water. We'd taken off our shoes and strayed from the bank of river stones to splash our feet at the gentle river's edge. I searched the water's edge for coins but didn't find any. I guess it wasn't a place where wishes were made.

Edward cupped a hand of water to toss at me. I flung my foot to spatter him with the cool river water. Killdees called out as they chased us along the riverbank. We were soon exhausted and collapsed on a park bench overlooking the water to air dry our feet and legs. I laughed at Edward, his hair windblown from the harsh air blowing across the river. As we caught our breath, we squinted our eyes to look far across at the neighboring state of Arkansas.

"It's as if we were looking across the continent," I said.

"This is my favorite spot in the entire city," Edward said. "Do you have a favorite spot you like to go to?"

"I have several."

"Take me to one. Let's go now."

I thought of Bachardy Park. It was my escape, my church, my refuge. I've barely known Edward two days, and I just wasn't ready to share that place with anyone else. I don't know if I'd ever share it with anyone. Sometimes we need somewhere only we know.

"I could take you to lots of them, and all at the same time," I said.

"Do you have a magic carpet to take us to all these places?"

"Nope, but I do have a camera."

My apartment was still very spotless and intact from the night of my house cleaning frenzy. I would take Edward to my apartment and share my photos with him. This may not be the time to tell him about the park, but it was a good time to share my hobby with him. I had a feeling he would appreciate it.

And he did.

I can't say I've had many friends, besides Sallie, over to my apartment to show them my photo albums. None actually. Even with Sallie, I never dragged out the albums for fear of boring her with them. Guests pretend to be interested in that kind of stuff, but they really aren't. You might as well pull out the projector and subject them to old home movies without sound. I felt different about Edward. I really felt like he would take interest in them, so I took a chance and showed him.

"You're really good at this, Blaine. Did you take a class?"

"Not one lesson."

"Do you develop them yourself?"

"No. I have my own personal developer who does them for me."

"Wow!"

"The pharmacy on the corner."

He laughed.

With photos, someone always has to pick a favorite, no matter if you tell them to or not. Edward's was a photo I had forgotten about, taken several years ago when I was shooting downtown. It was a picture of a downtown intersection with a café on the corner and a street car coming down the street. People were busy coming and going up and down the sidewalk and crossing the street. I had taken the picture from the rooftop of the building across the street, so it was a nice aerial view of what was happening down below on the ground.

"Have you ever heard of Christopher Isherwood?" Edward asked.

I was stunned he had asked me that, and overjoyed. I immediately stood up and walked over to my bookshelf across the room and pointed to two shelves where all of Christopher's books were kept.

"Heard of him? I've read every word the man has written!"

I couldn't have wished for anything better we could possibly have in common than Isherwood.

"This picture reminds me of the cover of *Down There on a Visit*. Not the original cover I'm sure, but the current reprint edition that you can find in any bookstore. Is that the one you have?"

I ran my finger along the row of book spines, searching for the book. One of my favorites. The cover was a sepia toned photograph of an intersection in Germany. The Nazi flags waving on the sides of the building definitely postmarked the picture. And there was a café and people on the street. There were buses in the background in place of my streetcar. Edward held the book in one hand, comparing it to the photograph in his other.

"Did you do this on purpose?" He asked.

"No. I had never thought of it until you said something now."

"Isn't it strange how our mind is capable of retaining and using information at times we aren't even aware of? You probably looked down off that rooftop and saw this downtown scenario and snapped the picture without giving it much thought, but inside your mind was telling your eyes that you were engrossed in this because you'd seen it before. You liked it. It reminded your brain of something that you enjoyed."

"You really believe that?"

"Of course. I bet you find yourself quoting Isherwood, don't you?"

"All the time. Well, I want to but I don't really do it out loud. I mean I may have said it out loud once before, but his sentences do pop into my head from time to time in different situations."

"Exactly. We can relate his writings to our everyday life, and you don't quote him out loud because you don't think anyone else gets it. And they probably won't. I doubt Sallie is well versed in Isherwood."

"She isn't."

"So you don't say what you want to say out loud. But you think it."

"I do."

"Isherwood wrote about the war. He wrote what he saw. It inspired him."

"And Isherwood inspires me," I said.

"Therefore, he inspires your photography, whether you know it or not. I'd love to have a copy of this one, if you don't mind."

"Take that one."

"Are you sure?"

"I want you to have it."

I walked over and sat next to Edward to help him remove the photograph from the album. He had said all the right words and something told me this was the perfect time to kiss him. At any other time, I would have sworn he had a hidden tape recorder in my room, even in my head, which gave him the information he needed to be able to say the things he just said. I knew that wasn't possible.

Edward understood me. There was no background check he could have performed, no list of my eccentricities Sallie might have armed him with. Or was there? I had spied on him at the University, but that did not supply me with any pertinent knowledge about him that I could use to gain his trust. I didn't learn anything there that I wouldn't eventually find out after I met him. Did I?

There was no cheating at this. This was real. It was a genuine moment developing between two people, assuring them they were glad they'd met each other. Two pieces of a puzzle had finally come together for us.

The album slid off his lap and fell to the floor as I wrapped my arms around his shoulders to kiss him. Passion, yes I said passion, quickly raised the temperature in the room as we fell into one another across the sofa.

I liked the scratch of his facial whiskers against my jaw and neck. Biting at his pouty lips, I explored the ridges of his teeth with my tongue. He was still with his arms open as I explored his mouth, neck, and ears with my tongue. I lay there on top of him awkwardly having my way with him. I wished he would wrap his arms around my back, caress me and kiss back, anything. I didn't want to be completely in control. I was accustomed to taking control and getting what I wanted when I brought some guy home from happy hour, but I wanted this first time with Edward to be different.

I pulled back from him, but only long enough to peel off his shirt. He leaned up to help free it from his back against the cushions. Lying back down, he pulled at my shirt and lifted it over my shoulders. I admired his flat model-like stomach and the fuzzy blond trail of hair that encircled his navel and disappeared into his jeans. The soft hair repeated itself around each of his large nipples, but the rest of his chest was tan and smooth.

I couldn't resist. I took one of his nipples in between my finger and thumb and gave it a soft pinch. That was usually the spark that ignited sexual adventure in any man. Edward was no different. He let out a silent grunt and bit his lip. I grinned at his reaction my move had instigated. Without wasting any more time, I leaned down and took his nipple into my mouth and gently sucked it. This was the intimate connection that he needed to open up.

As I bit at his tit, Edward arched his back like a cat. He wrapped his arms around my back, pulling me closer to him to interfere with my mouth while gently pressing his nails into my flesh. He pushed the palms of his hands down my sides to my pants and slid his hands inside. As he cupped my bare buttocks with his strong hands, I stopped the attention to his nipple and fell against his shoulder. Admiring the splash of large freckles across his collar bone, I wished this night would never end.

Forty

Despite being both emotionally and physically satisfied, I awoke in the middle of the night just the same to check my alarm clock's position. I awoke the next morning at 5:32am and went about my usual AM ritual. With my mind still a blur, I locked my apartment and traced the numbers on the door, I counted the steps as I ascended downstairs, and I counted the walking steps to the coffeehouse.

Even standing across the street from the shop, waiting for the traffic light to indicate it was safe for me to cross, I failed to notice that the shop was dark and Sallie's car was not parked at the side entrance. I crossed the street in tune to my usual cadence, ready to face whatever that work day handed me. Digging into my pockets to find my key, I reached for the door handle and caught my reflection in the glass. Focusing my eyes to look through it, I noticed there were no lights on inside. Sallie was not bent over the pastry case stocking it with muffins, a routine also emblazoned into my memory so hard, but my memory didn't trick me into seeing her like the maple tree.

She was not there.

For only a second, I feared the worst. She could be lying on the floor inside having tripped and fallen and knocked herself out, or worse, she had been robbed. Or maybe she had just slept late and had yet to arrive. On any other day, I would have rushed inside and looked for her, afraid of the condition I'd find her in, but I saw that her car was not there. I would have still hurried in and called her, awakening her from a deep sleep as I had done once before, flipping switches and lights and prepping things in a mad dash before the morning crowd arrived. But something clicked and told me today was not a day to worry.

It was me whose schedule was all misaligned.

"We're closed today," I told myself out loud in a whisper.

For once, I found myself in a single inconsequential moment in my life where my schedule was in disarray. Me, who timed and counted every step he made, every breath he took, every hour he slept, every second that ticked away, had come to work on a day when there was no work to be done. I stepped back from the door to admire The Latte Da, its doors closed to customers on this one day of the week. The punch clock and time cards, the espresso machine, the coffee beans were all latent and still. Even the world outside was still in bed and not craving caffeine.

I laughed at my reflection in the glass of the door. I spun around and laughed loudly into the air, not caring who I might awake. I was a man on a mountain top, having scaled the highest peak. I was a sprinter first at the finish line waiting for second and third to catch up. I was an old man with the winning BINGO card. A thousand moments of triumph rattled the globe everyday, but I was too busy counting sidewalk blocks to see them.

My victory came today, in the form of being somewhere I didn't have to be and not even knowing I was going there. I stepped to the curb and peered down the empty street. There were no spectators there to cheer me on. No congratulatory bouquets of flowers. No applause. Only a red stop light that blinked fifty times a minute (yes, I had counted). A bird on a power line scolding my laughter. And silence.

There was no humming of electricity surging through the streets and buildings, no wind blowing, no blood coursing past my ear drum. Just the silence. Pure silence because for only a brief moment the aching madness inside my head, that controlled my every move like puppet strings, had stopped.

"Do you like the opera?" Edward asked me that afternoon on the phone.

"Are you joking? I love the opera," I lied.

I don't know why, but when you are falling in love with someone you suddenly start to crave things you never liked before. It's sort of like being pregnant. Or you lie about such things because you know they like them. I'd never been to an opera, but if Edward wanted to take me to one then I would certainly go just to experience something new with him. I wanted to spend as much time as possible being with him.

Forty-One

"So you think that by making out with Edward, it's somehow curing you of your obsessive compulsiveness?"

"Yes I do."

On Monday, I told Sallie about the events of the weekend. I told her what had happened with Edward on Saturday at my apartment, and then how I had showed up to work the next day.

"But I've done that before. Your mind is just busy and thinking about other things, or it's your usual routine to want to go there," Sallie explained.

"In my case, I never forget. When you are obsessive compulsive, those mistakes don't just happen on their own."

"Well, imagine what will happen if you guys keep dating. You'll probably be completely cured. They'll write about your sex life in medical journals years from now."

"If we keep dating? Why wouldn't we keep dating?" I asked, intrigued by her comment.

"You guys just met. I mean I'm glad you guys seem to be getting along, but you never know how things are going to turn out weeks, or even months, from now. You might get bored with each other. I hope not and I wish you the best, but that's just the joy of dating, right?"

I didn't know. This was the first time I'd really seen someone longer than one night.

"I think we will be together for a long time," I said, trying not to let her blasé comments rattle me.

I didn't know why dating was suddenly so casual for Sallie. Were she and Charlie having problems? Was their connection in jeopardy? Each of us had both wished for longevity in our love lives. Why would she jinx that now with such comments? I really wanted to believe that Edward was my cure.

I know it sounded strange, which is the only reason I knew I could tell Sallie and not have her laugh at me. I had never been officially diagnosed with obsessive compulsiveness. What I knew of the mental illness, I had researched on my own. There has been a bitter feud over the cause for years. On one side is a group who believe that obsessive-compulsive behavior is a psychological disorder. They believe that OCD is caused when people believe they are personally responsible for the obsessed-crazed thoughts they experience. This exaggerated sense of responsibility makes sufferers more anxious, keeping the distressing thought in their mind. They try to avoid this feeling of responsibility by performing compulsions, like I do.

On the other side are scientists who believe that obsessive-compulsive behavior is caused by abnormalities in the brain. I believe it's a little bit of both, but the exact cause still eludes scientists today. Centuries ago such mental illness was believed to be caused by the devil, and the only cure was an exorcism. If the devil was in me, why the hell would he make me count and memorize the number of steps it takes me to walk anywhere?

So, why couldn't sex be the cure? Back when I was fumbling with boys in the bathroom at happy hour, I was never like this. The illness only popped up when the one night stands stopped. My brain craved the sexual attention, and when there was none it forced me to forget about it by clogging my mind with routines, numbers, and schedules. Only I didn't forget about it. The compulsions just took up the time that I should have spent trying to get out and meet someone.

My happy hour trickery only satisfied a need temporarily. At the end of the night when what's-his-name had got off and left, I'd fall asleep satisfied. That was only a physical satisfaction. In the morning, I'd still wake up alone. The hole in my heart, craving companionship, was still there, aching so much it made me sick. And maybe now that I had met Edward, that hole was slowly being filled in.

Meeting Edward was curing two illnesses.

"Sallie, can I ask you something else?"

"Oh, I don't know. Next you'll be asking me if I think your photography cures something."

"Only boredom."

"What do you want to ask then?"

"Is Auden gay?"

"Do you have to ask?"

"Yes. I don't really know."

"You have the worst gaydar. Maybe sex will cure that too."

"So he is?"

"Why haven't you asked him?"

"Because gay people don't ask other gay people if they are gay or not. Like you said, most have good gaydar and already know. And besides, there's always that one chance you got it wrong, and then that person is embarrassed or develops a complex over why you thought he was gay in the first place. Or he thinks you are hitting on him. Or he might even beat you up for asking. So no, I'm not going to ask him."

"Auden would never hit you."

"Just tell me. Is he gay or not?"

"I'm more curious about why you are asking."

I hated when Sallie played this game with me. Of course, she knew that at times the question I'd ask really had some other deeper question behind it. This question was no different, but I really did just want to know for sure if Auden was gay or not. Call me stupid for not knowing already. Call me stupid for having to get a second opinion.

"Do you like Auden?" Sallie asked.

"As a friend? Yes. As a coworker? Yes. Nothing more," I said with impatience.

"Are you sure?"

"Yes," I stressed with a hiss. "I am sure."

There was a long pause while she contemplated her answer.

Several customers came through so I had to busy myself at the espresso machine making their drinks while Sallie bagged pastries for them.

"Well?" I asked when the customers were gone.

"I still want to know why you have to ask."

"I was going to invite him out one night with me an

Edward perhaps. There. Are you happy?" I was lying. I had to think of something quick to hopefully get an answer out of her and to end this train of questions.

"I don't think I've ever heard Auden actually label himself as gay or straight."

"Sallie! Sexuality is not a label. It's not a pink triangle or a Star of David. It's not a Rebel flag, not even a rainbow flag for that matter. So, don't start that label shit with me. Does Auden suck cock? Does he kiss men? Does he take it up the ass? I wish you would just tell me already." I was screaming in a loud whisper even though there were no customers in the shop.

She turned beet red. A contagious giggle sputtered out of her, and we both began to laugh. We laughed so hard we couldn't breathe. I fixed us both an iced coffee to cool off. Sallie was ignoring my stare, attempting to look busy wiping down the front counter. I stood there, looking at her, with my hand on my hip still waiting for an answer. Finally, I walked over to her and put my hand on top of hers to stop her from cleaning.

"Well?" I asked.

"Auden's heart yearns for a man. There, I said it. Happy?"

"Thank you."

And with that, I lifted my hand from hers and walked away to refill the beans in the espresso machine.

Forty-Two

I know what you are thinking.

Auden.

If things don't work out with Edward, now I have a back up, right?

Wrong.

I don't want to picture Auden in that light. So many gay men are quick to wash their hands of one lover and pick up another the very next night. That's the way I acted back in the days of being a bathroom sex junkie. That's not love. That's not the volatile feelings you get on the inside when your heart starts racing every time you think of that special someone.

And I doubt Auden would fight for my love. Sallie had already said he wasn't the fighting kind, and two men competing for my companionship sound silly. But ever since that night Auden and I sat down across from one another in the coffee shop to peruse my photo albums, I couldn't help but get the sense Auden was interested in me. Maybe I'm just being facetious. After all, we all want what we can't have. You can be a single man forever in the mad gay world and no one will pay attention, but as soon as someone does give you a second look everyone starts vying for you.

But it's not really you they are after. It's your suitor. It's the lucky guy who reached out to that single unsuspecting someone, tugging on their heart strings. Everyone is thinking, "why didn't he pick me?" So, all the men set out to change his mind, snarling over him like mad hungry dogs. I was afraid that might happen with me and Edward. Neither of us was really the wooer, unless you count Edward kissing me first. I somehow sensed I had nothing to worry about with Edward though. His eyes would remain focused on me, and no other man could steal his love away.

I also felt Auden could probably be just as faithful. But Auden is a coworker. What if it didn't work out between us? One of us would have to leave the coffee shop. It's never good to be coworkers with the one you love. Neither of you could come home and tell the other how your day was because both of you got through it together.

Together. That's an odd word if you think about it.

We all want to be together with someone. We want to experience things together. Share bed and board together. Eat together. Sleep together. Take trips together. Together also means your stable and well-adjusted, in sync, well-balanced. You've got it together, which makes me think that by getting together with someone (finally), I am also getting myself together.

And so I am standing at a split in the road in the deep forest of my life. I'm just a few steps down the path where timing took me. The path where Sallie met Charlie, who knew Edward, who was introduced to Sallie, who introduced me to Edward, who just so happens to click with me. And just as I said yes to the blind date, just as I turned to take the path to the left, the trees cleared a little and showed me what could be waiting down the path to the right.

Tempting.

We miss out on a lot in life without even knowing what we missed out on because of the path we chose. We have to keep moving forward, and years from now when our paths have curved or led us in opposite directions, we might stop and turn around to see where we've been. It's too late and too far to go back, but we can't help but wonder where that other path would have taken us.

No coin in a downtown fountain can change the truth we wish for.

Forty-Three

Months passed. Without asking, Edward bought us tickets to a charity ball and auction at some downtown hotel. I had walked by the hotel almost every time I got on or off the bus when going to Bachardy Park, but I had never gone inside.

"Do you have a tux?" Edward asked.

"I don't even own a suit."

"I'll rent one for you. What are your sizes?"

"Medium, I guess," I said with a shrug.

"No! What size shirt do you wear? What length of pants?"

"Medium," I said again. I didn't know.

"Have you ever worn a tux?" Edward asked, walking behind me and checking the collar of my shirt. He mumbled some numbers to himself, committing my sizes to memory.

"Of course, at prom in high school," I said. I was lying. I didn't go to prom.

Without asking, I brought my camera with me that night. Edward made it a point to make me feel uncomfortable about it, even more uncomfortable than the tux already made me feel.

"You aren't bringing that in with you," He said in that parental tone I hated.

"Why not?"

"You'll look like some kind of a reporter."

"What am I supposed to look like, besides an out of place penguin?"

"You're my date," he said.

"And dates aren't allowed to take cameras?"

He said nothing. I left the camera in the backseat of his car. He parked in a shady garage across the street. I wanted to put my camera in the trunk if he wasn't going to let me take it in, but he said it'd be fine. The hotel was an elaborate palace of gold and red. I felt like I was trespassing. I'd never seen a place so beautiful. I stopped to admire things for as long as I could, committing all of my shiny surroundings to memory since I didn't have my camera.

The charity event was to auction local artwork to raise money for the children's hospital. It was not the colorful and expressive art I was accustomed to after having been around Auden and the art school crowd at The Latte Da. Old men with young sparkly women gathered around a chunk of marble under glass, transfixed as if they were trying to telekinetically get the junk to move. It made me laugh. Edward gave me an evil eye to be quiet, and then dismissed himself to get drinks for us. After he left, a woman in a red sequined dress shunned me for leaning against a black bricked column.

"Young man, that's art," she snuffed.

"Only because someone told you it was and wants to charge you a thousand dollars for it," I said back.

She rolled her eyes and pranced away.

Edward came back and handed me a watered down drink he'd also probably paid too much money for. I tried to hold back a yawn, but he caught me.

He had taken me to operas, and foreign films with subtitles, baseball games with just us and Charlie, and to Broadway musicals. These were events my social life had not even dreamed of, outings I'd never wished for. Were these the types of things gay couples were supposed to do together? I faked a smile of excitement when he announced that he'd bought us tickets to the matinee or some French circus that was in town. They were always his places and his ideas of things to take us to. I had none.

My one place was Bachardy Park, but after the long list of shows and movies he'd treated me to, my one idea had no hope. Edward would probably just laugh at it, and so I never mentioned it. I preferred the nights we went out to dinner and then just came home to a bag of microwave popcorn and a rented movie, then sex. Those were the only nights I felt like we were a real couple, no matter how boring that might have seemed. On those other nights, I put on a tie for Edward. It wasn't even my tie. I didn't own a tie. I had to borrow one of his. He'd pick me up and straighten the tie in the car for me before driving to some cathedral to listen to an all boys choir. He'd smile with content at whatever he had turned me into for the night. I'd roll my eyes when my back was turned, like a kid dreading Easter dinner at Grandma's house.

I must have done a good job at covering up the boredom because Edward never questioned it. Was he blind to my boredom or was I just that good of an actor? I didn't want to be. Relationships often mold two people into something much different, as we adapt to the likes and dislikes of our close one. It's 50/50 for both people. Give a little, take a little. Or it should be, right? But I didn't feel like Edward was doing that. Was there any substance at all to my life for him to adjust to? I was a rented date on his arm at those charity events. I had no parade of my own.

And I soon learned that I was nothing more than his project. He said it himself one night on the way home.

"Aren't you glad you met me? I bet you never did these kinds of things before," he said to me.

I didn't answer him that night. He didn't ask me to. Just once, for maybe only a second or two, I wished I'd never met him.

"Do you want to go?" He spit at me now as I stood their sipping the weak beverage he'd handed me.

"No, I'm fine. But I did notice almost every other person in here has a camera," I bit back.

He dangled his keys in front of me, a signal that I could go get my camera out of his car if I wanted it. I did. But I also wanted to just catch a bus and drive away from this place. This whole night was so not me, and I was doing a rotten job of pretending it was.

The shards of glass that twinkled on the concrete next to Edward's car confirmed I shouldn't be here. When I peered through the broken window into the back seat, I suddenly knew what a parent must fill like when their child goes missing. My camera was gone.

I ran to the front gate to ask the guard about the security cameras. Conveniently, the one on the level we'd parked on was not working. I ran out to the sidewalk like a lost man cursing the heavens. Frantically, I paced back and forth. Strangers walking by stayed clear of the crazy man in the tux. I started across the street to go back into the hotel, and then stopped. I was so mad at Edward right now that I wanted to hit him. Instead, I decided to walk the few blocks to Bachardy Park.

I didn't know if walking alone downtown at night was safe. I'm sure muggings and robberies at gunpoint were so frequent and so routine that the news didn't report them anymore. I put my wallet in my coat pocket just to be safe. I didn't know if you could go into the park after dark either, but I did anyway.

All was quiet and still, except for the trickle of water in the fountain. I dug in my pocket and found an old penny I'd picked up outside the hotel because it was on heads. Edward had rolled his eyes at me for stopping to pick it up. I usually picked up coins on the sidewalk if they were on heads or not. I wasn't worried about luck. Those coins were wishes no one knew they'd lost, tooth fairy dreams no one would go look for. But I needed some luck tonight. I needed my own wish to come true. So, I flipped the coin over the banister listening for its plop in the water. And that was it.

I looked up into the dark night. The angel at the top was hidden in a sky of black. No wind rustled the leaves of the trees and bushes. I imagined a hundred beady black eyes opening and peering down on me from the limbs up above. Pigeons and squirrels called one another whispering and wondering why I was here at this hour, and where was my camera?

Where was my camera?

Forty-Four

"I'll buy you a new camera. I'm insured," Edward said.

He didn't get it. It wasn't that easy. Offering to buy me a new camera was great, but it would not fix the damage that had been done. My camera would have never been stolen if he'd just let me take it in with me when we got to the hotel.

I wanted to believe that when he walked away to get us drinks that night, he'd gone to his car and staged the whole thing for some odd reason. He'd broken his own car window and hidden my camera in his trunk. Maybe he'd keep it hidden from me for a few days, and then miraculously present it to me as if he was a fireman pulling a cat from a tree for a little kid. I'd take it from him and hug him and call him my hero. I wasn't going to be polite and dismiss his offer out of kindness. He was going to replace my camera.

"Okay, let's go now," I said.

"Now?"

"Yes, you can buy a new camera for me today."

"Don't you have a birthday coming up?"

"Yes, but Sallie gave me that camera, the one that was stolen from your car. I've never gone 24 hours without it since she gave it to me. So, we are going camera shopping today."

I loved making him feel guilty about it. He should.

At the store, I could tell Edward thought we should be able to pick out a camera like a gallon of milk, check out, and leave. Oh no! Shopping for a camera was like shopping for a new car. These things take time.

"What about this one?" he asked, pointing to a cheap snapshot pocket size camera, the kind I hate.

I refrained from commenting on his choices, but I should have said something. The price tag of that model was less than one hundred dollars. The camera Sallie had given me costs almost six hundred.

"I want one exactly like the one I had."

"You should get something new," Edward said. "How

about this one?"

Again, another cheap model made of glossy yellow plastic. It was also water proof. I closed my eyes so he couldn't see them rolling.

"I'll take that one," I said to the clerk. I pointed to the exact model I had before which was locked in a glass case behind the counter.

"That camera costs six hundred dollars," Edward said.

"You're insured," I replied.

"Fine. Get it. Let's go."

"Not so fast. Now I have to pick out a case and memory cards. I'll need some batteries too."

"It doesn't come with those things?"

"Nope," I said.

If he had not been paying for this, I would have preferred he didn't come with me. I know it's sad to say that about someone you are dating, but Edward always wants me to go everywhere with him. If he needed to go get gas for his car, he'd waste gas coming to pick me up first so I could go with him.

"You can keep me company," he'd say.

I was accustomed to doing things alone long before I met him, so for a while, I never asked him to go anywhere with me. I was content on doing it by myself. Also, when I was alone, I didn't feel as uncomfortable about counting blocks of concrete in the sidewalk or how many steps it took to get somewhere. Eventually, I started asking him to accompany me to the grocery store or to the pharmacy. I did it to be nice, since he always asked me to go everywhere with him. I also did it out of selfishness because he had a car, and I thought he might drive us there instead of me having to walk.

"I'll just wait here at your apartment and watch television. You won't be long, right?" He'd ask.

When you keep telling them no, sooner or later a dog learns to stop doing whatever you don't want them to do. He didn't make me feel like a dog, but it only took two or three times of Edward saying no before I just stopped asking him along.

The only thing different between my new camera and the

old one was the way the battery compartment opened. I never thought my old camera needed an improved battery cover, but apparently someone in a camera company somewhere thought it did. And it was indeed a nice improvement. I did, however, choose a totally different case for it. The one I had before was discontinued.

"You should get this black one. It's nice," Edward said. It was also marked fifty percent off because the strap was missing.

I chose a brown leather case with extra pouches for filters, batteries, and accessories. It added another hundred dollars to our shopping spree price tag, but Edward never said a word about the total when we checked out.

"Test it out. Take my picture," Edward said outside.

He straightened his shirt, checked his teeth in the rearview mirror of his car, and asked how his hair looked. I felt like a fool standing there while he primped. I laughed to myself with the thought of the camera breaking when I snapped his photo.

"Be sure to print a copy of that for me if it looks okay," he said in the car as we drove away.

I'm sure it looked just fine. I'd left the lens cap on, purposely this time.

Forty-Five

"Just forget about it," Auden snuffed at me when he asked me if I had given any more thought to the photography contest. My reply was habitual and not thought out, just a common response to someone asking you a question when you aren't totally listening. I had replied with, "What contest?"

I knew exactly what contest he was talking about. How could I forget? Honestly? Ever since I had met Edward, it was as if nothing else around me mattered. At work, I was just going through the routines to get to another five o'clock on the punch card so that I could leave and go spend time with him. I rarely knew what day it was unless it was the weekend.

Do you know the feeling when you are so absorbed in new love that a month passes you by in the blink of an eye? Then, there's always something that wakes you up, something that smacks you across the jaw and snaps you out of it. With gay men, it's usually a one month anniversary. I know that seems trite, but it's very true. Few gay men see a one month anniversary, much less one week. One month is one year in gay years. Edward and I didn't celebrate with cake and candles when we reached that milestone, and as a matter of fact, two months had passed before anything brought me back to real world consciousness.

It was Auden asking me about the photography contest. I had only three days left to submit an entry. Snap! Suddenly, I realized there had been something else before Edward that I had been looking forward to with great anticipation. Should I just submit the pigeon girl picture and be done with it? With the pressure mounting and the deadline approaching, would I be able to shoot anything else that would be worthy of a win? Since I met Edward, we had practically spent every night together after work. How would I find time between Edward and work to shoot photos?

"I'm going to be a little late," I said to Edward on the phone. "Sure, everything is fine. I just have a few quick errands right after work. Mind eating late? Pizza is fine. I'll call you when I get home."

I didn't lie to Edward, except I had no idea how this was going to be quick. I had not been to Bachardy Park in almost three months. Before, I went almost every other day and I always spent at least two or three hours there. It was never quick. Bachardy was my menagerie, my safe place, my sanctuary. If I was planning on making a quick trip out of it today, it would be a waste of photos. I could only hope fate had something extraordinary waiting for me when I got there.

And it did.

Forty-Six

I had left the coffee shop and walked half way down Madison Avenue before I even realized I had walked right past my stop where I usually catch the bus to go downtown. I even looked up and saw that very bus passing me now. Like a parent ushering kids to the corner on the first day of school, I waved to the bus. It was a tired and slow wave, not really a wave at all, but more like a hand drawn into the air for some teacher to call upon me for the answer to a question. But I was the one with the questions.

Was Edward worried because I had called him to tell him I'd be late? Did he think maybe I was seeing someone else behind his back? Would he be upset if I didn't come over tonight at all? If I didn't, this would be the first night we'd spent apart from one another since a week after we first met. Should I just go to him now and forget about the photo? Should I forget about the contest all together? Would Auden be mad at me if I did? He'd probably never speak to me again.

Instead of catching another bus, I walked the rest of the way to the park. It had only taken about twenty minutes to get this far, so I figured another twenty minutes of walking would get me to the park. Wrong. It only takes about twenty minutes by bus to get downtown. It was an hour before I made it to Bachardy on foot, and by the time I got there I was exhausted. I collapsed on the first park bench I saw and laid down on it to curse myself for being such an idiot.

I still had about thirty minutes of light judging by the sinking sun. I looked around and the park was empty, save for a few pigeons strutting around a half eaten bag of peanuts on the ground. Even the squirrels were already at rest in the trees, probably looking down at me and mocking me for missing out on something profound that someone else had probably caught on film right before I got here. A chorus of katydids started up in the trees and broke the odd silence.

I laid down on the nearest bench with my arm across my

face, contemplating why I had even come here today. I felt like a weary shopper standing in an empty store, forgetting what I had even come in to buy. From the corner of my eye, I spot an elderly man with a cane hobbling into the park on the opposite side. He walks with short wobbly steps, taking his time as if waiting for someone or something to catch up with him. I can't imagine anything walking even slower than him, but I can only see him from the waist up. His cane is in one hand and as he walks past a few low bushes I notice a leash in the other. He probably lives in one of the nearby high rises and brought his dog out for a late afternoon stroll.

Pigeons fall in behind the man and as he reaches a bench in the middle of the park in the clearing, I notice a bag of bread dangling in his hand next to the cane. The birds recognize him and strut behind him in an odd parade, eagerly waiting for him to reach his bench. There are some pigeons flying in to sit around the bench, knowing the exact place where the old man is going to sit down. I remain low on my bench to avoid his attention. I have tons of photos of folks feeding birds in this park, but you never know when there just might be one that's different. That's the magic of photography. You aim to capture one thing, but often come out with something totally different you weren't expecting.

As the old timer reaches his bench, I catch him speaking to some of the birds like old friends. The pigeons flock around him as he turns around and eases himself down onto his seat, propping his cane up close to his leg. With the bag of bread between his legs and shaky hands, he fumbles with the twist tie. Birds flutter as he opens the bag and takes out a piece of bread. Leaving it whole, he throws it to the ground to appease them and to get their attention off him while he takes out another piece to crumble up into smaller bites.

As I lay there watching him, I had forgotten about the leash. It catches my attention when I notice that a dog has not accompanied the old man into the park. Instead, he has brought a cat. I can't say I've ever seen a cat on a leash, and the birds certainly don't seem to mind this one. With the leash around the old man's wrist, the cat leaps up onto the bench to sit next to him. It eyes the ball of feathers and wings on the ground in front of it, but without threat. The cat looks to be older than the man. It is sickly thin, and its matted white hair looks as if a preschooler cut it with a pair of dull scissors. It licks a paw and then teethes a piece of bread offered by the old man.

I silently finger my camera out of my bag like some sort of spy. Hoping I don't need the flash, I set the camera to sport mode so I can take continuous pictures just by holding down the button. I hold it to my eye and search for the elderly man in the viewfinder as best I can while lying on my side. I like the look and feel of him in the distance before me, the low shot of him, and the limbs of some bushes in the forefront offer a nice frame around him. I zoom in on the cat, finished with its bread and back to contently cleaning a paw. Birds flicker in sync with the shutter of my camera, but I don't think these shots are contest worthy.

It's odd how when you are falling in love, nothing else matters. We lose interest in the beloved hobbies that kept us content when we were lonely. We are bored with the things that were there for us from the start. The magic of being the camera has worn thin.

With the camera in my face, I am blind to anything outside the view finder. A dark lanky figure has darted into the park from the same direction the man came from. The old man does not seem to notice, as the pigeons still have his full attention and he still has half a bag of bread. Not even the cat notices someone in the distance coming toward them. I don't even notice until the person walks into view of my camera. It startles me. On instinct, I pan the zoom back for a larger view just in case a crime is about to be committed.

Looking over the top of my camera, but still aimed and ready to capture any photographic evidence that might be useful later, I detect the old man is in no danger. But I am shocked at who I see. It's Auden. He speaks to the man who raises his head to acknowledge Auden with a slow toothless grin. I hear Auden ask if the man has seen anyone with a camera. He's come looking for me. While Auden's back is to me, I roll off the bench and to the ground since he is taller and would probably spot me if he looked in my direction. Staying low to the ground, I still have a perfect view of them through the bushes. I prop myself up on my elbows to watch.

Auden asks if he can sit down. The man gestures to the end of the bench and meagerly pulls the cat closer to him although the cat doesn't move. Auden sits, exhausted with a look of hopelessness. He offers a timorous finger for the curious cat to sniff. The old man assures him that Pretty Kitty is harmless. I find it odd that the old plain man is not shaken by the look of Auden. In his black striped pants and sleeveless tee revealing arms sleeved in tattoos, with his oily spiked hair and black eye shadow, he and the aged man are complete opposites. They sit in silence and watch the birds.

With an outstretched trembling hand, the old man offers Auden a slice of bread. At first, Auden declines but the man insists and just as he reaches to take the bread, I snap the picture I knew I had come here to take. Unstaged. Unrehearsed. It's that kind of slice of life I live for.

Auden breaks the slice of bread into a few large pieces and tosses them all on the ground at the same time. He smiles at the old man and then gets up from the bench to walk away. The birds flit at his feet, anxious for him to get out of the way so they can finish devouring the bread. He starts to walk away, going back the way he came but he stops. I see him fidgeting with the pocket inside his vest. I knew the fountain was calling him. It does that to everyone.

He walks over to it and pauses, not touching the black iron barrier. He looks into the water almost meditative-like. With his thumb, he flips a coin into the air and over the water. He turns to walk away, not watching it clunk through the wet surface and sink to the bottom.

I wonder what he wished for.

Although tempted, I kept my hand out of the fountain that day.

Forty-Seven

, I never revealed myself to Auden in the park, nor did I ever tell him at work that I saw him looking for me. I decided to leave that up to him, but he never mentioned it either. Wondering what he wished for, if anything at all, burned in my head when I saw him at work. Having to face Edward was a different story.

He was waiting for me in the parking lot of my apartment when I returned home from the park a few hours after sunset. I had stayed on the ground until Auden left shortly after I had taken his picture. Once Auden was out of sight, I still waited a few minutes so I didn't chance us ending up on the same bus back to Midtown. I assumed he would take a bus back to Midtown, but I didn't know if he lived there. He could have lived only a few blocks away from the park for all I knew. The old man was soon out of bread and waddled away tugging at Pretty Kitty's leash. The sun was gone, and the sky was turning from powder blue to cobalt.

Although I'd never had a boyfriend, I could still sense Edward was not happy with me. His arms were crossed as he leaned against the back of his car. His mouth was drawn to the side in a tight smirk. He had every right to be mad at me for having not called him yet. He even glanced at his watch as I walked up to him, as if he'd been waiting for quite some time. I didn't have a watch, so I had no idea just how long it had been.

"Hi," I said.

"Where have you been?"

"Sorry I haven't called yet."

"Where have you been?" he asked again.

"I can explain."

"Explanations are usually lies. Just tell me the truth, Blaine." I didn't like his scolding mother-like tone.

"Let's go inside. I'll tell you the truth."

"Save me the walk up and just tell me now. Here."

Gay men are notorious for losing their temper when they

have no control over where their lover is. And most routinely presume the other is out cheating. Men are so untrustworthy, and therefore also distrusting. I'd never had a lover to lose my cool with, so I was unaware of what that feeling was like. Judging by Edward's conduct, I'd say he was well versed in this feeling of unease. Until now, it was only something I'd witnessed among squabbling couples at a bar. I knew that no matter what I said, it would all sound unconvincing. This feeling of interrogation didn't help.

I don't know who counted how many words a picture is really worth, but I knew there was a reason I always left the date and time setting on when I took pictures. The choppy orange letters in the lower corner could always be removed before my photos were downloaded. Lucky for me, I had not erased them on the bus while riding back to my apartment. Without another word muttered, possibly pushing Edward and me deeper into an unnecessary argument, I flipped the camera on to view mode and handed it to him.

"What's this?"

"Just take a look."

"How do I know this is real? How do I know you didn't set it to that time as an alibi?"

"Because it's today. It is real, and I'm not that sneaky. I have no reason to be," I bit back.

No one had ever accused me of lying to them about anything. Never. I didn't like being accused now.

I was beginning to wonder if it would always be like this between us. This was our first argument, if you counted it as an argument. I did. I counted it, simply for the fact that Edward had questioned my word.

"Sorry. Guess I overreacted," he said. The smirk on his face faded to a shy little grin and his cheeks blushed red the way they did the first day I met him.

Like water off a duck's back and every other cliché used to insinuate ease, the tiny conflict between us was over. But some part of me on the inside was still torn. I wanted to be mad at him because he'd stolen my joy. Leaving the park on a day like today with my camera in tow was like a natural high for me. Pure happiness. Coming home to Edward in my parking lot made it all fade away.

"Why didn't you tell me on the phone you were going to take photos of Auden?"

"Come inside. I'll explain."

Upstairs in my apartment, we sat down on the sofa and I told him about the contest deadline. I showed him the other pictures I had narrowed it down to. He watched as I erased the date on the pictures in my camera and uploaded them to my computer. We both agreed the photo of Auden and the old man was alluring. It was much more fascinating than the others, even more than the pigeon girl.

"That was nice of Auden to pose for you," Edward said.

I took my chances and left it at that.

We ordered a pizza and devoured it in minutes. I'd never licked tomato sauce from the corners of another man's mouth before, but the make-up make out session between Edward and me that night was just as tasty. I'm sure it put Edward's mind at ease that yes, I was still his and I wasn't cheating on him. My feeble life still revolved around him and I needed him to be a part of it to even exist.

I bit his nipple since I knew that was *the* spot. I pulled his hair. I pinned his arms to the bed. I fell between his legs and teased him with my tongue, sucking him nice and slow and bringing him close to climax. Then, I would back off and start over again. Edward preferred it fast and hard, fucking my face with the thrust of his hips, but I wouldn't let him this time.

He growled with excitement because I'd never acted like that in bed before. He thought he was turning me on, but more and more he'd begun to turn me off. My romp tonight was sort of revenge. It was punishment for him for his accusations.

It was "I told you so."

Forty-Eight

Isherwood often wrote about himself in the third person, recounting experiences from his diaries, but he always let the reader know it was him. In his writing, he considered himself as a separate being, a stranger setting out on an adventure. He'd tell the reader that he'd revised opinions and maybe even changed the accent and mannerisms of this being. In his writing, he could be someone else. He could be whoever he wanted to be. But it was still him. He could be anyone else and the reader would never know. We'd think he just made it up or was writing about someone else he might have known, but why lie about it?

I knew exactly how he felt.

With Edward asleep in my bed, I routinely woke up at an odd hour in the early morning. I opened one eye to check the time on my alarm clock on the dresser. Sensitive to the eerie red light that can fill a room at night, Edward had turned my clock around to face the wall so that we could make love in the complete dark. I see the red light of the clock shining on the wall. I carefully crept out of bed and walked over to the dresser. The alarm on the clock is not set because it's the weekend and I don't have to work in the morning. For no reason, I unplug the clock and watch its digital face fade to black. I tip toe to the bathroom and close the door.

The bathroom is plunged into total darkness as I shut the door without a sound. I have no choice but to turn on the blinding light above the medicine cabinet. I turn my head, away from the light with my eyes shut tight, and flip the switch. I open my eyes slowly and blink several times to adjust to the now brightly lit room. No matter how much you expect for the light to come on, your pupils still sting. I take a piss and then turn my attention to the mirror above the sink.

Despite the puffiness and crusty eyes, despite the tussled hair and the whisker burn on my cheeks from making out with Edward, I don't know this face in the mirror anymore. But I like it.

I think about 32, but I don't feel the need to wash my hands three times and dry them twice, or to realphabatize the medicine cabinet although I know nothing is out of order. Nothing is out of order. It never really was. I just concentrated so hard on making sure it didn't get that way. When I step outside the bathroom, I don't think I'd count the number of steps back to bed although I already know it's eight. I've counted it time and time again. Eight steps. Eight steps back to a man, gently sleeping in my bed, who puts his arm around me and holds me close on his pillow.

There's a peck at the door. I open it slightly, not wanting to blind him from the light. Edward is standing there naked with heavy eyes.

"Is everything okay?" he asks.

"Yeah, everything is just fine," I reply.

"Come back to bed."

I flip out the light and open the door the rest of the way. I try to move my feet forward to follow him to bed, but they won't move. I must have stood there for several minutes in the dark because Edward called out to me again.

"Just a second," I call back.

I can feel a cold sweat breaking out across my forehead. I know what I have to do, no matter how much I don't want to do it. One – two – three – four – five – six – seven - eight. I've made it to the bed. I pull back the covers and crawl in next to Edward's warm naked body. In the darkness, I feel him against me growing to attention. I want him again. I want him inside me, but I just want to lie there. I turn over to spoon with him, scooting my body closer into the curve of his hoping he gets the hint. He does. I hear the sound of spit as he coats his fingers. I try to relax despite the awkward push of him against the back of me. Eventually, my muscles loosen and accept him. His rhythm is slow, gentle, and constant. Like a hypnotic metronome, my mind starts to count. One – two – three – four – in – out – in – out – nine – ten…

This is not going to be as easy as I thought.

Old habits die hard.

Forty-Nine

I called the art college on Saturday to double check the contest deadline for turning in photos. I had until mid-afternoon on Sunday to submit my entries. I learned there were multiple categories and that each person could submit up to three photos as long as none of them were in the same category. I decided to submit my cemetery picture in the Statuary category, and luckily there were two different categories for people: one for photos of just children and one for adults. So, I could submit the pigeon girl photo, and the photo of Auden with the old man.

Edward and I went to brunch at a local hotel restaurant. Then, we went to the pharmacy to have my photos printed. To be submitted, they had to be 4x6 photos, glossy or matte and dry mounted on 11x16 white canvases. They also had to be framed in plain black frames with no mat.

"Do we need to run by a craft store or frame shop?" Edward asked at the pharmacy like a parent asking their forgetful child.

"Nope. Just go back to my place now."

Edward was amazed that I already owned all of the supplies to prepare the photos as needed.

"You're really good at this," he said.

"I guess so. It's just a hobby."

"I don't think you give yourself enough credit. You really should do this for a living."

"I draw a paycheck at the coffee shop."

"But why not get paid to do what you love the most?"

"I don't know. I've never given it much thought. If I had to call this work I'd probably get tired of it. If what we do is fun, they wouldn't call it work, right?"

"I guess I see it differently," Edward said.

"How so?"

"If you love to do something so passionately, you don't have to consider it work at all. It's just more of a joy to get paid doing it. Don't you think?"

"I guess so. I guess I'm just afraid of failing."

I had actually given a career at this lots of serious thought. I just hated these pep talks from Edward. They were so rehearsed since he was a teacher. They rolled off his tongue like any parent or coach giving a boost of encouragement. I hated it.

"You are past that point. You are a successful photographer. Your work shows it. You just need to take the next step."

"I don't know if I have time."

"Time? You spent all your time either taking photos or slinging coffee and bagels before you met me. You've got plenty of time."

Before I met him, he says. Before I met him I liked who I was. Sure I had my faults and my eccentricities, and I still have them, but I miss that person now. I didn't like the person Edward was turning me into. And over time spent with him, I had slowly come to the realization that I didn't like Edward either.

"I don't know where to start," I said, filling the air with words I didn't mean. I wanted to just get him to shut up about it, but I wasn't doing a good job at it.

"Take a professional class. Get a degree or get certified. Get some business cards made and go freelance at first. I could help you," Edward said.

I was still hesitant. I appreciated Edward's gusto, but I just couldn't convince myself to pursue photography full time. I really liked my job at the coffee shop and I knew that Sallie depended upon me. It was a comfortable part of my life and routine, but maybe that's the problem. My routine. It was boring. I needed to take chances and risks. I needed someone like Edward to push me.

Being a professional photographer was a lot like a second grader standing in front of the class and telling their classmates they wanted to be president. Kids always dream of a glamorous job because they have yet to know what "work" really is. Instead of asking kids what they want to be when they grow up, we should ask lil Jimmy how he plans to support lil Jenny over there when he knocks her up on prom night because their school didn't offer a sex education class. Instead, they were too busy writing essays about being doctors, lawyers, and firemen.

No one wants to be a factory worker, trash collector, or even a coffee barista. We sugar coat our kids' lives with popsicle dreams so much that the meaty slap across the face from reality is a harsh wake up call. Jenny wanted to be a pharmacist, but with the help of her parents now raising their granddaughter and because they sued to garnish dead-beat Jimmy's wages as a construction worker, Jenny goes to night school and flips burgers at the Snack Shack.

Failure. It's not the lack of succeeding at what we set out to do until we give up on doing it. I wasn't giving up on becoming a professional photographer because it was never a dream I reached for. I was content with selling caffeinated beverages and praying for good tip money.

I don't remember what I really wanted to be when I grew up. I'm thirty-two years old, and I'm still growing.

Fifty

I know what you are thinking.

Blaine will win the first place prize in the photography contest. He and Edward will move in together, and he'll start taking photography classes in pursuit of opening up his very own photography studio.

Right?

Shit. That's the happily ever after ending you only read about in novels. That's Edward's dream. Not mine. I've already told you. Although there seem to have been some lapses, each and every day of mine follows a strict pattern. Every time I break the routine I pat myself on the back for stepping outside the box, whether it was done intentionally or not. But in the back of my mind, there's some small part of my brain that's worrying about the consequences I might have to endure just because I didn't count steps this time or I had cold breakfast on a hot breakfast day.

Consequences.

They can change everything, including what I've set up here for you as a no guess happy ending. I know. I know. I spoon fed you this cutesy lil romance story, and it's probably not fair that I'm about to tell you how it all goes astray. I'm even warning you that it's going to get off track. But I don't like surprises. And remember. Obsessive compulsives don't like change, especially when it fucks with their routine.

So blame me.

Blame me for telling you now that shit is about to happen. Blame me for fucking this entire love story up by not sticking to my routine. Blame me for all of it. But you have to agree. I could just stop telling you this story right now if it was some cookie cutter romance. You'd already know what happens on the rest of the pages, if you haven't already fallen asleep by now. No need to waste my time or yours. But just when life gets boring, the way we like it, things change. And we don't always like those changes, but we have no control over them.

You still don't know all you need to know.

Fifty-One

Nobody dies.

Therefore, there is no mystery to solve. So even though it's my opinion, I can share with you the one single thing I like to believe caused all of the following events. An unsuspecting nail in your tire caused it to go flat. The bill got lost in the mail so you forgot to pay it. Every problem can somehow be narrowed down to one single origin.

Tribulations with romance work the same way, but they don't always have an easy solution. Someone is bound to get their feelings hurt, and so such evils are the worst kinds of problems at all. You can fix a flat. You can pay a late fee on your bill or beg for sympathy from the collector. Hurting someone's feelings leaves a permanent scar. Sure. They can forgive you. They can say they forget. But the scar remains, no matter how much we try to cover it up. We remember those things we tell others we'll forget. We let forgiveness tuck them into no more sleepless nights. But we do remember.

It all started that same day just after Edward and I had finished preparing my three entries for the photography contest. Without being rude, I got him to shut-up about me pursuing photography professionally. I did it by not answering him. I busied myself with the photos while he talked it all out of himself. And although it seems impolite, I think he might have asked me a question at the end. He might have even asked if I was listening to him. But I wasn't.

Inside my head, I had just shut him off and every word he spoke might as well have been an annoying song on the radio playing in the background. I wasn't listening. He stood over my shoulder for a few minutes as if waiting for my reply, only to discover that I indeed wasn't listening. So, he went and sat down on the sofa.

When I was finished with the photos, I asked him if he was ready to go to the college. He stood up and mumbled yes very placidly and then walked right out the door and down to his car. I knew he was upset. My resolution was to just ignore him and let it all pass. Edward's solution would be to play the same game by ignoring me.

I locked my apartment and was just about to trace the numbers on my apartment door like always, mainly for luck this time. I pulled my hand back and decided instead to break the routine. Baby steps. Baby steps. Edward didn't speak a word to me in the car on the way to the college. He sat in the car while I went inside to sign up and turn in my entries. I was glad to be done with them even though the deadline was Sunday afternoon, and I could have spent all of Saturday working on them or taking more photos. I was content with my submissions and now it would be up to the judges. Edward drove us back to my apartment in silence.

"I need to run some errands. Call me tonight if you want," he said in the parking lot.

And so it was to be this way today. He was dismissing me. This was his excuse for not wanting to be around me the rest of the day. I knew what he really wanted to say was that he was pissed at me and needed some time alone. His way of saying it was just to evade the argument I had already been avoiding. That was fine by me. I had not had a weekend day to myself since we met. The time apart would be good for both of us. So, I played along.

"Oh, okay. That's cool. I'll just hang out here today," I said stepping out of the car.

Edward sped away without saying another word. If you were watching a movie, right now you'd question whether or not I'd ever see him again. Now c'mon, not even I'd know that yet just standing there.

So this is what anger feels like when you are in love, I thought. Pride gets in the way of love when there are two people who always think they are right, never wrong. So of course, I stood there questioning if I really was in love with Edward. Did I really want to see him again? Did I want to go through something like this every time we shared differences? Right now the answer to these questions was no. Maybe the time away from

him would change that. Maybe it wouldn't.
I didn't wish to know either way.

Fifty-Two

I needed to cure my Sallie withdrawals. It had been weeks since we'd spent anytime together outside of work. As luck would have it, her shift was almost over at The Latte Da, and she was pissed at Charlie for some hetero reason that girls get mad at boys.

"Let's go have a drink," she said.

"You read my mind."

Auden was silent and trying hard to ignore me even though there were no customers for him to assist at the counter. He busied himself pretending to check his syrups, cups, and lids; but I knew that Sallie wouldn't be leaving if everything wasn't already stocked for the evening shift. With only Auden working at night, Sallie's rule was to keep things stocked to prevent him from having to go into the stockroom and leave the front counter unattended. In the coffee business, there was no planning for a busy night unless the weather outside was cold.

I waited in the lobby for Sallie to gather her things.

"I turned in my photos today," I said to Auden across the counter.

He hesitated, probably contemplating whether he was going to talk to me at all or not.

"Which photos did you submit?"

He avoided eye contact with me, studying the pastry stock.

"The pigeon girl, the cemetery photo, and a photo from Bachardy Park," I said.

"Good luck," he said with a nod and walked away just as Sallie came out of the back office.

"Are you ready to go?" she asked me.

"Absolutely."

"If Charlie calls, Auden, tell him I've gone out with Blaine," she said.

"Will do," Auden replied. "Should I tell him where?"

Sallie looked at me, pondering her answer to his question.

"Don't bother. We don't even know where we might end up tonight," she said with a grin.

I liked the sound of that.

And with that, she grabbed me by the hand and pulled me out the door like a scarecrow on a yellow brick road. With the bell on the door ringing behind us as we left, we were off to find what the evening had in store.

Like old times, we first hit the college bars for cheap beer and snacks. We spent several hours and several rounds of beer at a pub table in the corner munching on mozzarella sticks and jalapeño poppers. Both of us avoided the topics of Charlie and Edward for as long as we could, although both of us secretly knew they were all we wanted to talk about. It felt good to get the anger out as we each shared a list of the likes and dislikes we had for our men. Sallie's list of likes about Charlie was much longer than my list for Edward. Sallie noticed but she did not comment.

We were having too much fun, like we did before on our date nights, to question each other on the integrity of our relationships. I could tell Sallie knew I wasn't so happy. Her short-lived troubles with Charlie tonight were expressed as if she was a pouty little girl not getting her way. I knew that she'd go home tonight and eagerly wait by the phone for him to call, maybe even pick up the phone herself in a drunken stupor and wake him in the early morning to apologize and tell him how much she missed him. She'd be eager to see him again. I wasn't so sure I'd feel that way about Edward at the end of tonight. I didn't even feel that way now.

I don't know why.

We left the college crowd to go to a Mexican bar and grill we'd never tried before. It was called Engañar and it was open till three in the morning. They supposedly had the best margaritas in town, which were two for one after midnight on the weekend.

"I'm going to end it with Charlie," Sallie said after her second margarita.

I had lost count of how many beers she had before we

came here. The slurring of her words told me that she was extremely drunk and had no idea what she was talking about. After two more margaritas, she was dosing off at the table. I knew I needed to put her in a cab and send her home. The bartender was nice enough to call one for us.

"I'll be right back," I told the cab driver as I opened the door and pulled Sallie out.

I helped her up the stairs to her apartment, one hand cradled around her to keep her from falling while I held her purse and shoes in my other. Sallie was talking nonstop but all of her words were drivel and not comprehendible. I had already dug through her purse in the cab to find her apartment key to save time. Inside, I put her into her bed and prayed she wouldn't ask me to stay. I tucked her in and kissed her forehead, and I could tell by the look on her face she was almost out.

I crept away from the bed and turned out the light.

"Blaine," she yelled in the dark just as I stepped outside her bedroom.

"Yes?" I called out from the hallway.

"You just need to dance. You need to dance it off, honey. Just dance. Not for me. Not this time. Dance for you," she muddled before drifting off.

I left her purse, shoes, and keys on the kitchen counter with a note for her to call me when she woke up. I turned out the light and locked her apartment door behind me. The humming of the motor of the yellow cab, still parked at the bottom of the stairs for me, beckoned.

"She alright?" the cab driver asked.

"She'll be fine."

I knew what she had said about Charlie wasn't true. She loved him too much and had no reason to call it off with him. She often said things she didn't mean when she'd had too much to drink. It was the first sign that it was time for her to call it a night. But the last part she'd said to me about dancing was definitely not the alcohol talking. She was right.

"Where to now, buddy?" the cabbie asked.

"Back to Midtown for me. Do you know where the

nightclub, Backstreet, is?"

     "Sure do. Off Madison, right?"

     "Yep."

     "Boy, they open till six. Who gonna take you home?"

     "I live a few blocks from there so I can walk home."

     "Alright now."

     I needed to dance.

Fifty-Three

I don't know who was tipping the DJ that night, but I hit the dance floor as soon as I walked in and danced nonstop through at least five or six songs. Last call was at three. I still had an hour to drink so I stepped off the floor to feed my buzz. The smoke and blinking lights accompanied the alcohol in making my head spin. The room was crowded with silhouettes. Waves of small talk and the exchange of phone numbers blotted out the music in my ears.

"Hey there," a voice said, breaking the noise, from behind me.

I looked over my shoulder to see a stocky young man with a shaved head and dark skin. He looked like he was of Spanish decent, possibly even Asian mix with his creamy brown almond shaped eyes. His shirt was off. Beads of sweat speckled his large tight pecs. His nipples were the size of half dollar coins. I didn't notice his snow white smile because I was too focused on his physique.

He was about a foot shorter than me. Veins popped in his beer can crushing arms. He wore only tight black spandex shorts and combat boots. His legs were just as tight and muscular as the rest of him. Gym Boy was probably going to ask me where the bathroom was. Usually in the bar, guys only asked me for a light although I didn't smoke. I always wondered what made them look at me and think, "Hey that guy probably has a lighter we can borrow."

"Hey," I said back to him with my best ice queen face.

"I'm Randy." He offered a hand to shake.

"Randy?" I was stunned.

"Yeah," he said. "Were you expecting Pedro, Edgar, or Hernando? Something like that?"

"Pretty much," I said blushing. "I'm Blaine."

His handshake confirmed he was the Man of Steel.

"Damn," I said.

"Sorry. Sometimes I don't know my own strength."

"Show off."

Now Randy was the one blushing.

We talked for a few minutes and Randy confirmed he was half Asian and half Latino, but he was born in the states. With Geography lessons aside, Randy soon got to the point of why he had spoken to me in the first place.

"I was just about to call it a night until I saw you standing here," he said.

"Is that so?" I didn't believe him.

"You live close by?"

"Actually, I do. Just a few blocks away."

"You wanna go back to your place?" Randy asked.

"What?"

"I'm sorry. Too forward?"

"Not at all. I admire a man who knows what he wants and is not afraid to ask for it," I mumbled.

The alcohol was quickly catching up with me now that I had been standing still. I blinked a few times to catch my balance.

"Well?" Randy said to me. I must have been silent for too long.

"Yeah?"

"Do you want to go back to your place?" Randy asked again.

I tried hard to study the ramifications of this situation. I know. I should have been thinking about Edward. I should have been thinking that quite possibly this man's intentions were to rob or even kill me right in my very own apartment. Instead, the mix of beer and margaritas and whatever I had to drink here at the club had me concentrating only on the rising bulge in my blue jeans. Enticement had presented itself in the form of this hot bodied man standing next to me. My mind tried hard to squeeze out the words, "no thank you." My lips spoke something entirely different.

"Sure. Let's go."

Fifty-Four

End tables were turned over. Lamps and magazines spilled to the floor. The sofa cushions were thrown about. Randy was on me as soon as I took my key out of the lock and opened the door. He was not backing me into a corner to hog tie and gag me while raiding my apartment. Instead, he was kissing me wildly while ripping open my shirt. I was a rag doll in his grasp as he held me close to him, kissing my face and sucking on my neck and shoulders.

I found myself saying, "yes, yes, yes," out loud for two reasons. First, I was a talker when it came to satisfying sex. Edward hated that, and often shushed me. Second, I was happy to finally be with someone who wasn't afraid to take charge. I wasn't the one having to get Randy going. He had no problems starting on his own.

Our feet stumbled upon one another as he guided me through my apartment without focus. I felt like I was going to fall backwards so I constantly reached for anything within grasp and ended up knocking my furniture and belongings over instead. Finally, I gave into his advances and wrapped my hands around his torso as he pulled us into the bedroom.

The rest of our clothes, which had not already been pulled off, soared through the air and landed on the floor. The bed sheets would soon join them as we turned and thrashed all over the bed. Randy was like a wild jack rabbit, never once slowing down until both of us were completely satisfied. And even then, Randy still wanted more. Our lovemaking lasted the rest of the early morning and we finally collapsed in exhaustion just when the morning sun was peeping through the blinds covering my window.

I had never had sex, nor made love to a man if that's what you chose to call it, in such a capacity. Edward was a much gentler lover. He liked long sessions of foreplay involving massage and kissing. To me things like that are okay for the occasional weekend, but there are other times when I just really want to get down to business right at the beginning. Edward wanted every intimate moment between us to last forever, and so I often became bored with it just after ten minutes of kissing. Inside my head, I wanted to ask him to wake me when we got to the good part. I never said that out loud though. Suddenly, I had come to the realization that Edward bored me in bed. Sometimes we forget about what we are missing out on because we accept what we already have. We make ourselves believe that we are content with it.

I awoke just after noon. Randy had faded away like a ghost. What more is there to expect from a one night stand? I lay in bed for several minutes, either unable to or unsure if I should move. I was extremely sore from the acrobatic marathon of man-on-man action I had just woken up from. My head throbbed. My lonely clothes, mingled with the blankets on the floor, were a quick reminder that last night wasn't a dream.

I staggered out of bed and into the bathroom for some aspirin and a drink of water. After surveying the damage in the living room, I found only the light bulb in the lamp was broken. I began to piece the room back together when I found an envelope on the floor and sat down on the sofa to examine the contents. It was the greeting card Edward had given to me at the coffee shop that day just after we'd met. It was a wordy card about meeting someone new, walks on the beach, hand holding, stars in the sky, and the like. The way it made me feel now was a lot different than the way I felt when I had first opened it there in the bathroom at the shop.

The phone ringing behind me interrupted any oncoming trace of guilt. It was Sallie and something was wrong.

"Can you please come down to the shop?" she had been crying.

"What's wrong?"

"Someone broke in last night just after Auden had locked up."

"Is he okay?"

Silence, then Sallie broke into more tears.

"Sallie, is he okay?" I repeated.

"No!"

I quickly hung up the phone and headed toward the door, but thankfully noticed I was completely naked and had not even picked up my keys. Before embarrassingly locking myself outside in the buff, I hurried into the bedroom to retrieve some clothes. I found my keys on the floor and rushed out the door. Turning to lock the door, I looked at the number 32 there on my apartment door. Why hadn't I traced the numbers the day before?

Everything that had happened since that moment yesterday when Edward and I left to submit my contest entries came barreling back into my brain. Edward and I were mad at each other over something so trite. It'd been the first night we had spent apart from one another ever since we met. Sallie was mad at Charlie and went out with me instead. I had gone to the bar and brought someone home. I had sex with them. I had cheated on Edward. And now the shop had been broken into. Auden was hurt. Could all of this have happened just because I didn't trace my apartment number with my fingers yesterday when I left?

It was a simple task I had done every day when stepping out of my apartment. I reached up and traced the three with the index finger on my left hand, and then traced the two with my right. It was a step in the routine that seemed so trivial but I had done it everyday ever since I had developed this problem. Every silly manner I performed I did so because I felt I had to. There was no questioning it. It was as if my body would freeze in place and not let me go any further until I set and reset the alarm clock, counted steps to the bathroom, timed my shower, ate a cold or hot breakfast, left for work on time, and traced those gold brass numbers on my front door.

I could not possibly predict any outcome of not doing my routine. Up until now, I believed that breaking the routine was a step in the right direction. I was on my way to recovery just because I had been able to step away from the door yesterday without performing the task. Was I wrong? Immediately, my mind was blaming me. It had to be my fault. The magnetic pull of our fate in the universe had sent all of us spiraling out of control because of this. All because of something I had not done.

I reached up to trace the numbers now, pressing my finger hard against the surface of the three and the two as if I could somehow erase the mistakes that had been made. I wanted to wipe away these mistakes and go back to this place yesterday. By tracing the numbers now, no magical vortex opened for me to step into. No time machine appeared from the sky to rewind me into the day before. Everything outside was the same as it had always been. My mind would not let me believe that things could not have been any differently had I followed the routine yesterday or not. I told you earlier you could blame me. Blame me now too.

I was already blaming myself.

Fifty-Five

I raced down the stairs, careful to count all thirty-two of them to prevent anything else bad from happening. I needed to run as fast as I could to the coffee shop, but my feet would not let me. I concentrated instead on counting each and every step I took and noting each of the five blocks as I came to the next one. I soon broke into tears, unable to get to the shop any faster than my brain would let me. I felt like a mime against an invisible brick wall. The world around me was spinning out of control while I stood there, running in slow motion but not getting anywhere.

Spinning red and blue lights ricocheted off the sides of the coffee shop. I could see two cop cars and an ambulance parked out front. As I crossed the street and broke through a small crowd of people out front, I noticed shards of glass littering the sidewalk. The front door had been smashed in.

"What took you so long?" Sallie asked, grabbing my neck and pulling me into a hug when I came in the front door.

"Is…he…okay…" I tried to speak but was out of breath.

"He's going to be fine," an EMT said approaching us. "He's got a nasty concussion from the hit on the head, but he'll be fine."

Just then two more medics rolled a stretcher through the stockroom door. Auden lay there unconscious with several scratches on his face. Sallie pulled closer to me and buried her face in my chest. I watched through the broken glass of the front door as they loaded him into the ambulance.

"Did you want to go with him?" the medic asked.

Sallie looked at me with a questionable nod.

"Go ahead. I'll stay here and take care of things."

"I'll call you from the hospital," she said with a kiss on my cheek.

The medic helped her up into the back of the ambulance and then shut the doors. A siren announced their departure.

I turned to look around the shop. The dining room was

unscathed, but the waiting area from the front door to the counter was a mess. Glass littered the floor. The pastry case had been smashed in. The cash register was on the floor. Cups and supplies were thrown all about behind the counter. I approached the stockroom and office to look around. Several policemen were already back there.

"Sir, you can't come back here," one of them said to me.

"I'm one of the employees. Sallie, the owner, went to the hospital with Auden."

"What's your name?"

"Blaine."

"Were you working last night, Blaine?"

"No sir. I had the day off. I came in and picked up Sallie after her shift though."

"Got any idea who would do this?"

"No sir. I'm not really sure what happened. Sallie didn't say much."

"Best we can tell someone broke in last night after your coworker had closed down. They most likely thought the place was empty which is the reason for so much damage up front. They just wanted money and probably vandalized the place just for fun. Your coworker was in the back office closing up, probably heard the noise and got up to go see what was happening. He might have surprised them here outside the office. They beat him up a bit and knocked him out, then stole the money from the office and left out the back."

"Did they break into the safe?" I wasn't for sure why I asked that. Money was of no concern as long as Auden was okay.

"No, I don't even think they looked for a safe. Your manager told us you guys empty your till throughout the day, so they only got away with a couple of hundred dollars. Just the money he'd made last night."

"That's good."

"We're not done back here yet. You mind waiting out front for us and giving a statement later?"

"Sure. No problem."

I sat down at a table. It was somewhat dark because not all of the overhead lights had been turned on. Odd shadows from the morning light outside danced across the floor. My eyes were glued to the front door. Long sharp remains of glass, like teeth, jutted out the top and bottom of it in a strange spiral. It was my bizarre vortex I was looking for this morning, the door to either the past or future where I could change everything. I could not undo what had been done; I could only attempt to change what was yet to happen.

What else could have possibly gone wrong last night? I thought about Charlie and Edward and actually hoped they were okay. But then, I noticed someone at the front window, their hands cupped to the glass so they could peer inside. Of all people, it was Charlie. I didn't know if he could see me sitting inside, but I waved to him. He came to the door and peeked through the broken glass.

"Blaine? Is that you?"

"Yeah, come on in. Watch the glass," I warned.

"Sallie called me. Is everything okay?"

"For the most part, I think."

Everything wasn't really okay, but when someone asks us how we are doing today we always give a cookie-cutter answer and say 'fine.' That's because we don't know how to talk to one another. We don't know how to communicate. But that's the answer the questionnaire expects from you. If you took the time to actually tell them how lousy your day was, they'd probably never ask you again.

"She tried calling you here, but the line is busy. She thought maybe the phone in the back was off the hook or something. I told her I'd come down and check on you. Wow, this place is a mess," Charlie said stepping through the broken glass.

"They didn't get away with much at least. Did she tell you about Auden?"

"Yeah, and she told me to tell you that he's going to be okay. They took him downtown if you want to go see him. I told Sallie I'd drive you."

"Sure."

I didn't like hospitals. I couldn't think of a time I'd ever been in one since the day I was born. Maybe I was even a little afraid of them. Sallie had told me several times that I should seek medical attention with by obsessive compulsiveness, but I never listened to her. I know it seems silly, but I felt like I was carrying some big secret on my shoulders as we asked about Auden at the front desk. I felt like I was trespassing, like I was somewhere I wasn't supposed to be. My breathing began to speed up. Charlie noticed.

"Blaine, are you okay?"

"I'll be fine," I said, almost panting like a dog.

"Go sit down over there while I find out what room they are in."

I did as I was told, but the few steps over to the sofa seemed like a mile. The room began to spin like a ride at an amusement park. I knew I was about to go down. I leaned forward and attempted to throw myself toward the sofa for a soft landing. But when you are dizzy, things that often seem as if they are right in front of your face are usually still several feet away. I hit the floor instead. Its cold slap to the side of my face was actually somewhat of a relief.

I heard someone scream, although I had not taken notice of anyone else around me. Charlie rushed over and turned me on my side, peeling my face from the chilly comfort of the linoleum. I don't know how much time had passed before I came to. The aroma of bleach-like mint stung my nostrils. Through fuzzy eyes, I saw Charlie and a nurse standing over me. Charlie was holding a wet towel to my forehead. A nurse holding a small brown bottle stood over his shoulder. The look on her face was quite sour, as if she felt my pain from the awful smell emitting from the tiny bottle she'd just held under my nose.

"You okay?" Charlie asked.

"I'm a little thirsty."

The nurse handed Charlie a bottle of water. He opened it and raised it to my mouth. I took it from him, perfectly capable of giving myself a drink. I leaned up on my elbows and looked around at the few spectators who had gathered in the waiting room now to look at the silly queer who had passed out.

"How long have I been out?"

"About 15 minutes."

"Did you find out where Sallie and Auden are?"

"Yeah. I spoke with Sallie on the phone again. Auden is in a room now. He's sleeping and recovering fine."

"I want to go see them," I said leaning forward to get up.

"Are you sure? Here, let me help you."

Charlie and the nurse each took an arm and slowly eased me up to a sitting position. I tried to stand but the nurse told me to sit for a minute. The rush of blood through my body from the movement made me feel hot. I could feel my body adjusting its temperature and the feeling of light-headedness quickly passed. I finished off the bottle of water with hard gulps, savoring its icy feel going down.

They moved back and allowed me to stand on my own. I wasn't shaky at all. Someone in the room clapped. I gave them an evil eye. Was my quick recovery worthy of applause? Charlie took me by the arm and guided me toward the elevator. The doors opened and we stepped inside. We turned around to face the door and he punched the button for the third floor. I noticed the button for the second floor was already lit. 32. Charlie stood there looking up, watching the digital numbers above the door change. He was still holding my arm as the doors opened at the second floor. I envisioned seeing Edward standing there, reminiscent of that day at the university when I'd gone to get a look at him.

Instead, an elderly couple was standing there and smiled at us. The old man's smile faded as he looked down at Charlie still holding my arm. The old lady didn't notice as she slowly stepped forward getting on the elevator. The old man pulled her back.

"We'll wait for the next one," he said.

They disappeared behind the sliding doors and we rose out of sight. Charlie had not paid much attention to what just happened.

"You can let go of my arm now," I told him.

"Oh, sorry."

He pulled his hand away and immediately took a few quick steps to the right to put space between us, like a typical straight male.

"Make way for the homosexual invalid," I said under my breath.

Fifty-Six

In a soap opera like fashion, Sallie leapt from her chair next to Auden's bed when we entered the room. She rushed over to us and hugged each of our necks tightly. A few of her tears transferred to my cheek, but I thought it impolite to wipe them away.

Without a word said, she stepped aside for me to see Auden lying in bed behind her. She watched my face closely, somehow waiting for the shock to sit in or some tears of my own. It's the look you give an elderly person walking or standing on their own, when you are expecting them to possibly fall and you might have to catch them. The only thing that fell was a single tear from my right eye. It mingled down my cheek with what was left of Sallie's.

It was almost hard to see where Auden's make-up ended and where the bruises began. I approached his bed and secretly wished there were no bruises. His eye make-up was smeared from the corners of his eyes and down his face, like a crying televangelist's wife. One eye was swollen and a shade of deep purple. His cheeks were extremely red. He had a Kool-Aid moustache and his bottom lip was cracked. His black spiky hair was in disarray and some of the spikes looked messy and teased from where his heavy gel had worn out. The fairy tale characters tattooed on his arm were still smiling, but even they looked a little grim. Auden slept soundly.

Only those closest to you are ever allowed to see you behind the curtains of life, backstage in your dressing room hidden from the outside world. I'd seen Sallie without her make-up. She'd seen me plenty of times rolled out of bed unshaven when I'd spent the night at her place.

"Fairies must have danced in your hair last night," she'd say, commenting on the frizzy bush atop my head.

"They brought the house down," I'd say after seeing myself in the mirror.

Edward had seen me like that too, and completely nude.

I'd seen him too. At what point in our life do we trust someone so much that all of our gym class locker room fears are broken through and we allow someone to see us unbathed, unshaven, and unmade up? I guess sooner or later we force the bad upon someone who already likes us for the good. We assume they will accept us just the same, and they do. I've never heard of a relationship ending because someone didn't like the way their lover looked first thing in the morning.

But Auden didn't have that choice right here. It wasn't as if we'd all snuck into his bedroom one morning while he was sound asleep. If we had, I was pretty sure he'd look quite different. To myself now, I admitted I'd like to see what he did look like then. I only knew Auden as I saw him everyday at work. Greasy spiked hair. Dark make-up. Black and white clothes, tight and shiny. Black boots. It was his armor to face the world everyday. We all have some. Some wear it as clothes. Some just wear a tough skin on their backs. Last night, someone had forced their way through his armor. They'd hurt him.

In a way, I'd hurt him before too. Not for forcing my way through like a burglar, but for not looking past that armor when he was willing to let me in. He had wanted to let his guard down and to show me what was on the inside, but I'd ignored him and refused to look.

Fifty-Seven

"Any idea who did this?" a policeman asked. He had come to check on Auden and possibly question him if he was able.

"Not a clue," Sallie said.

The policeman handed her his card and told her to call him when she thought Auden was able to answer some questions.

We sat for what seemed like hours. Auden never woke, but Edward appeared in the door. My cold stare made him keep his distance, and if I had been the one in bed I'd probably thrown something at him if I was conscious. I don't think I was mad at him anymore, and I didn't know if he was mad at me. It just seemed fitting. A vase of flowers or a metal bed pan flying across the room could ease any tension. I smiled at him, unknowingly. He squeezed Sallie's shoulder and kissed her cheek. She took his hand and held it there for a second.

"How is he?" Edward asked.

"He's going to be okay," Sallie sighed.

The smile faded and my icy look turned to Charlie. He had called Edward, and I could only imagine what Edward had told him about yesterday.

"Want to get some coffee?" Edward asked me.

I didn't answer him. I looked at Sallie for approval and she nodded. I stood up and walked out of the room. He followed. Down an endless hallway of hospital white, we walked side by side in silence. He finally spoke.

"I need to apologize about yesterday."

"It's okay—"

"No, it's not okay. I got mad at you over nothing really."

"Well, I know what it was over—"

"Blaine."

Edward held a hand to my mouth. I wasn't intentionally trying to be difficult. That's just me.

"Please don't make this any harder for me than it already is," He said.

I pulled his hand from my mouth.

"Why does it have to be hard, Edward? Is it because you are stubborn and you don't think you were wrong? Is it because you think I should be the one apologizing but you know I never will? Is that it?"

"No."

"We had a tiff. It's not a big deal."

"It's a big deal to me."

"Why? Why is it a big deal to you, Edward?"

"I just think you don't give yourself enough credit."

I took notice that I had begun to raise my voice a bit. Luckily, we seemed to be the only two walking down the hallway at that time. We paused in front of a linen closet door, and I leaned back against the wall next to it.

"Listen, Edward, if this is ever going to work between us you need to learn to accept me for who I am. I don't have a need to feel successful. I like my life the way it is. I like to make elaborate coffee drinks for people and earn tip money. I like to go to bars to drink and dance. I like photography. I don't feel it necessary to exceed at those things. I'm content and happy with the way things are. I'm content with who I am, and anyone who dates me shouldn't try to change me. It just won't work."

Edward started to speak. Instead, he glanced quickly side to side. Upon noticing no one had joined us down the hallway, he grabbed me by the shoulders and kissed me hard on the lips. I put my hands on his waist and pulled him into me closer. I liked a man of few words.

I pulled away from his lips long enough to check the door beside me. It was a scrub closet and the door was not locked. Edward was busy sucking at my ear lobes, but I wrapped an arm around his neck and pulled him inside the closet to continue our love making out of sight. I was quickly reminded of the broom closet incident at the University, but I was careful enough to lock the door once we were inside.

We returned to Auden's room about an hour later with a cup holder holding four paper cups. Both mine and Edward's hair was a bit shuffled. My face was red from the burn of his five o'clock scruff. Charlie took a cup and thanked us. Sallie looked at me with a quirky smile and began to laugh. She laughed so hard she began to cry.

"What?" Charlie asked, unaware of the whole charade.

I just smiled and held back. Edward sat down, holding his coffee cup in front of his face as if using it for a shield to hide his embarrassment.

"Are you guys laughing at me?" Charlie continued. Dumb straight man.

"No, honey, we aren't laughing at you," Sallie said, patting his knee lovingly.

"But maybe we should be," I added.

Fifty-Eight

A couple of weeks passed before Auden returned to work at The Latte Da. He only spent a few nights at the hospital. But like a lot of victims of attack, a deep sense of paranoia set in. It was so bad that Auden tried to come back to work but he couldn't even man the front counter by himself with me and Sallie just in the stockroom. He would start to hyperventilate and break out into a sweat. It angered him more than it scared him. He wanted so badly for things to just return to normal.

"I want to do this," he told us with clinched fists.

"You need more time, Auden. Take all the time you need," Sallie said.

The physical scars had long healed. He now needed to tend to the emotional ones. And so he left. Sallie hired two part timer kids, regulars from the art college, who had asked if we were hiring. Both of them worked the night shift together because Sallie vowed no one would ever work alone at night again.

She let me train them. It was fun teaching someone the drink-making trade that just came naturally to me now after having worked here for so long. I don't remember the last time any of us had ever used a measuring cup or an espresso shot glass, but they were getting lots of use now from the new guys.

Taste testing was their favorite part. Like a child eating the very first batch of cookies they ever helped Grandma bake, their eyes lit up with excitement over their creations. Ah, to be young again. I didn't envy them.

Security cameras were also installed for everyone's protection. An extra tip jar on the counter collected donations from anyone who came in offering sincere apologies and asking about Auden. They wanted to help if we needed it. Sallie gave the money to Auden since she could not afford to pay him his full salary while he was off. I often threw in half of my tips each day as well.

Sallie also decided to close the shop an hour earlier at

night. It was the one hour of business she could easily afford to lose because it was definitely the slowest. Although the shop was sometimes full at that hour, we only rang one or two sales during that time if any.

I didn't like the changes, no matter how necessary they were. The progression of technology frightens me, even if it is to increase our safety. I can't help but think of the "good ole days" everyone likes to reminisce about back when there were dirt roads and no one locked their doors at night. Those days are long gone, but we can't stop talking about them. I'm waiting for the day someone builds a robot to make their coffee quicker, heck, to bring the coffee to their house because all of a sudden we've become too busy to talk to each other.

Pretty soon we'd be offering wireless and free internet service or a big chain bookstore would buy us out and move in with their bargain books and overpriced retail manufactured coffee. The world forgets about the shop on the corner because they want bigger and cheaper, they want to be wired or wireless, and they want name brands galore. They want to have what everyone else is having, and everyone else wants the same thing. Pretty soon our café is a sea of suits glued to their lap tops and Wall Street Journals, talking on their cell phones, drinking drab coffee, and reading cheap books.

I bitch about it because it affects the one thing in my life that I enjoy doing everyday the same way I've been doing it as long as I've worked here. But there's always some angry customer, or some scientist, who wants to find a way to help me do my job better. But all he ends up doing is eliminating the one part of the job he thinks is unneeded: me. Sure, there's better ways of communicating, better ways of travel, and better ways to run warehouses and corporations. I can't imagine the world without computers, and even my digital camera is a huge advance in the technical world. Go invent those things though. Leave the coffee alone.

I know it seems odd that a simple security camera hanging on the wall, slowly pacing back and forth over the shop, watching our every move at the shop could cause me to stress out like this, but it does. I don't think Sallie cared much for it either. She wasted so much time in the office eyeing the monitor on her desk as if she were waiting for someone to attempt to rob us again. She practically sat there with the phone in her hand and her finger on the speed dial button to reach the police.

Just a few weeks had passed when Sallie's phone rang one night. She had invited Edward and me over to join her and Charlie for dinner and a rented movie. A phone ringing in the night and the caller ID announcing it was the shop made all of our hearts leap. Sallie swallowed hard and grabbed the phone.

"Hello," she practically whispered into the receiver.

"Who is it?" Charlie asked.

Sallie ignored him as she listened closely to the person on the other end who obviously had a lot to say. Sallie nodded her head repeatedly, saying nothing.

"What's wrong?" Charlie asked.

"Shhhh," Sallie said to him with a finger to her lips.

I stood up, worried that something had happened again. I waited by the door, ready to bolt to the car if we needed to go.

"Thanks for calling me. Go ahead and close for the night and lock up if no one is there. Check the tape when you are done cleaning up and then call me and let me know if you can see them on it clearly. And be very careful not to erase that tape. Thanks."

She hung up the phone and looked at us.

"What's up?" I asked. My own patience was wearing thin.

"That was Jake, one of the part timers. A customer alerted him that two guys right there in the shop were bragging about breaking in and beating up Auden. He thinks they are students from the art college and he's seen them in there before," Sallie explained.

"Did he call the cops?" Charlie asked.

"No, there was no time. They weren't there very long after the customer told him. He's going to check the security tape and make sure we got them on camera."

"Let's go," I said.

"Shouldn't we wait for him to call me back?"

189

"We're five minutes away. Let's just go."

All four of us piled into Charlie's car and he drove us to the shop. Sallie knocked on the front door before letting herself in with her key. Jake was wiping down the tables. He heard the knock and came over to let us in.

"We got 'em," he said.

Fifty-Nine

Although he didn't care about going down to the police station, Auden let us take him so that he could pick his attackers out of a line up. Other students later came forward to confess the two guilty boys had told them things in class. Their plea was not a vendetta against the shop at all, but one against Auden personally. They had also been responsible for the vandalism of a painting of his that had hung at the school. They didn't like his artistic point of view.

Auden chose not to press charges against them no matter how much we told him he should. Instead, Sallie gladly went after them for what they'd done to the shop. The boys were sentenced to six months at a teen correctional facility for breaking into the shop, theft, and for vandalizing school property. They also had to pay for all damages and a portion of Auden's hospital bills.

"I don't want to make their record any worse," he said.

"Look what they did to you," Sallie said.

"I'll heal. They have to live with this the rest of their lives."

And he did heal. Auden soon returned to work and all three of us were back to our regular routine. The security camera continued to watch us from its position high on the wall, but it didn't bother me as much anymore since Auden's case was closed.

Auden dismissed the whole thing as artistic differences. He even laughed at the thought that two boys beat him up because they hated his art, or because they were jealous of his talent. His story made front page news. AN ARTISTIC HATE CRIME, it read. Sallie wanted to frame the story and hang it on the wall of the shop, but the camera was already a constant reminder to us of what happened. Auden just wanted to forget about it and move on.

I guess time heals a lot of things. Despite the small bump in the road, Edward and I had not changed much. We still spent every night with each other. We made love almost every night and sometimes two or three times a day on the weekends. It was the best mental medicine I'd ever had despite not being happy with the way he treated me like a child sometimes. His need to take me to places and events so I could experience new things every weekend was a regular part of the routine by now. I'd become so accustomed to it just like any part of my regular everyday habits.

With someone there to occupy the empty space and time in my life, I soon stopped the obsessive counting. I still traced the numbers on my apartment door every time I left or came home, only because I blamed Auden's accident on me not tracing them that one day. But I tried not to see that as a sign that my obsessive compulsiveness was still around.

"You really believe having a boyfriend cured you," Sallie said.

"I do. Getting laid all the time is great, but he always has us on the go anytime there's a free moment. I don't have time to think about old habits anymore."

We slipped off for drinks after work one night. I called and told Edward where I was and that I'd be late. He didn't mind. He knew how much my friendship with Sallie meant to me. She was a big part of my life long before him, and I always hate when people lose sight of their friends when they are in a relationship. Friendships are much stronger, and you will definitely need them one day. Edward never argued about me hanging out with her. I called him because I knew he hated not knowing where I was at any given moment, but he wasn't as vocal about it as he had been. He was learning to trust me. He had no reason not to.

Well, there was one reason. But you can't really call it a reason, yet, if he doesn't know about it, right? Fate, luck, coincidence or karma, or whatever you choose to call it, has a funny way of catching up with us when we don't want it to. Even though I had cheated on him that night, I had washed that dirt from my hands only because it happened as a result of our first real argument. Everything that happened before that argument I had tucked away and only saw our relationship blossoming from the moment we made up going forward. We'd started over, so that night didn't count. Did it? There are no spaces in time or between the blocks on the calendar. No markers. No time outs. Only the ones we try to put there, and no matter how much we try, we know they don't really exist. It's just our way of remembering things, or choosing to forget them.

Sooner or later, I'd have to go back and face it. Edward would have a reason, and its nasty little head would reveal itself at exactly the not-so-divine moment when I least expected it. Just when you feel your life is back on pace, there hasn't been an argument, no flat tires along the road to wherever your life is taking you, that's when life decides it's time to mix things up a bit. A problem forms, like a nasty pimple popping up on your face at the wrong time and in the wrong place.

I tried not to obsess about it. I ignored it like an angry bill collector. I smiled at Edward and he made me smile. But in the back of my mind, I knew our days together were numbered. No wishing could change that.

Sixty

I didn't want to go to the bar that night, but Edward insisted. It had been years since he'd been to a gay bar, and he never had any desire to go until tonight. He knew that I liked to go before I met him, and had not been out since then as far as he knew. I knew he was just trying to do something nice for me. He wanted us to have a night out. Maybe I had missed going out. We actually went out all the time. We went to movies or out to dinner. We did other things besides the bar like couples should do, but tonight he thought we should go have some drinks and dance. He yearned for non-stop bass music and a disco ball spinning over a crowded dance floor. Secretly, I yearned for it too but I knew it was too dangerous.

As I've mentioned before, club-going gays usually like to continue going to the bars immediately after meeting someone. It's their way of showing off. They've seen the same slow faces every night of their life, and it's time to tell them all that they've found someone. Eventually, there's a night out that's pretty much your going away party. You settle down and possibly buy furniture together. You lose all interest in the bar and whatever it has to offer. After meeting Edward, I just stopped going out all together. There was no reason to show Edward off to everyone because I didn't know a lot of those people. He had never gone to the bars here before I met him, but for some reason he was eager to go now.

I tried to ignore him and should have created a diversion. Instead, we sat on the sofa in silence watching the television. I was at one end of the sofa and he was at the other. I didn't look at him, but I could feel the weight of his eyes on me. I should have been elated that for once he was asking me to take him somewhere. That had never happened before. Our weekend destinations were always predetermined by him and way in advance.

"Well, what are we going to do?" he asked.

"What would you like to do?" I asked, finally turning my

head to look at him almost with a sense of guilt. I faked a yawn hoping he might think I was too tired to go out.

"I want us to go out. Isn't there a club just down the street? We could walk."

"Yeah, we could walk. Do you really want to go?"

"Yes, I want us to go out. Let's do something different. You've been there before, right? I've never been so take me. It's safe, right?"

I wanted to lie and tell him that it wasn't safe. In all the years I'd lived in this apartment and gone to that bar, there had never been any crime in this neighborhood. We had no worries of anything happening as far as our physical safety was concerned, but I felt that our relationship would not be as fortunate.

Maybe I was overreacting. Maybe I was feeling a little jealous, and I didn't want to "share" Edward with the other gays at the bar. I didn't want to expose him to that element; I was afraid he might succumb to the beat and leave me for the club hopping lifestyle. I knew that sounded ridiculous, and was just a crazy excuse not to go. But it could happen.

"Let's have a drink before we go," I said.

Although I had built myself up to expect for us to have a terrible time, the bar was actually fun with Edward. I somehow expected Edward to turn into a little kid at an amusement park, bright eyed and ready to take on everything. Instead, he was very reserved and stuck to my side; maybe he was even a little afraid. We got another drink as soon as we got there and stepped out on the patio to people watch. At first, I tried to look bored and hoped Edward wouldn't want to stay long. That was when he asked me if I wanted to dance.

There was something much more thrilling about dancing with someone who you'd already slept with prior to that night. Usually, I had yet to know their name. Our close suggestive dancing teased each other and helped build up our libidos, like some odd insect dance that's part of a mating ritual. With Edward, it was different. I didn't have to work hard to impress him. Instead, we casually enjoyed each other's rhythm with no anticipation of getting laid. We already knew who we were going home with. For a moment, I was glad we had come here.

Edward's attention was drawn to a man dancing on top of a speaker box with his shirt off and eyeing me with a huge grin. When I saw that his eyes were focused on someone or something, I turned to see what it was. My eyes met the man's. His smile grew and he waved a hand at me. I nodded at him and smiled slightly, then immediately turned back to Edward who was trying hard to read the expressions on my face. I smiled at him and shrugged my shoulders, letting him know I had no idea who the man was, even though I did. His name was Randy.

I knew as long as we stayed on the dance floor, Randy would not approach us. He was showing off up on the speaker box and he wouldn't want to lose his dance space by getting down. The music was so loud that he'd be unable to speak to us anyway, and he knew that too. My legs were getting sore and I wanted to sit down but I refused to stop dancing. That's when Edward had to take a piss.

"Come with me," he said close to my ear.

Without waiting for my reply, he took me by the hand and pulled me off the floor. I prayed Randy had focused his attention on someone else. In the bathroom, I stepped up to a urinal to relieve myself. Edward was pee shy so he went into one of the stalls. I stared straight ahead to the wall but could see Randy out of the corner of my eye stepping up to the urinal beside me.

"Hey man," he said to me.

I turned to acknowledge him. He had stepped back far enough to flash me. He unzipped his pants and pulled himself out, waving it at me. He was definitely high.

"No thanks, man," I tried to whisper. I turned my eyes back to the wall and hoped Edward could not hear.

"That's not what you said that one night," Randy said.

"I'm not interested tonight," I whispered sternly, zipping myself back up.

"What? You didn't like it?" Randy asked.

I was just about to step away and hoped Edward was finishing up so we could get out of here. That's when Randy reached over and grabbed my crotch. With his other huge arm, he pinned me against the stall wall and planted his lips onto mine. The force of his kiss was erotically familiar. I missed it. It caught me by surprise but he was too strong for me to pull away. I tried, but it was too late. Edward had stepped out of his stall and saw us in the mirror.

"Excuse me," Edward said.

Randy stopped kissing me and looked at Edward.

"Hey man, what's up?" Randy said.

"I was just about to ask you the same thing."

"You into three ways?" Randy asked, still holding me to the wall and fondling my bulge.

"Three ways?"

"Sure. My friend here and I had a wild night a couple of months ago. We were thinking about giving it a go again tonight. You wanna join us?"

"Is that true?" Edward asked me. I had remained silent until now.

"Not about tonight. He came onto me. That's all," I said. I was afraid of making Randy mad enough to punch me.

"That's all? That's not what you were saying the night we tore your apartment up," Randy spit into my face. The smell of booze was heavy on his breath.

"When was this?" Edward asked Randy.

I hope he'd get it wrong. I tried to cut him off. "It was—"

"It was about six weeks ago," Randy said interrupting me. "You guys sure you aren't up for it tonight?"

Edward didn't say anything else. Instead, he turned and walked out of the bathroom.

"What about you then?" Randy asked turning back to me.

"No thanks," I yelled. I managed to pull myself away from him and went after Edward. Upon stepping out of the bathroom, I expected to find him standing there waiting for me, but he was gone. In the crowded room, I was standing there alone.

I walked through the bar once, looking for him, and checked the patio. He was no where to be found. If I had found him, I don't know what I would have said to him anyway. I'm no good at apologies, and the bar wasn't the place for them anyway. The walk back to my apartment was unhurried and daunting. At the end of the street, I looked across to my apartment's parking lot. His car was not there. Edward was gone.

I climbed the steps to my apartment, counting each one as my foot made contact with it. I stood in front of my apartment door for a long time just staring at the number 3 and 2 on the door. I outlined them again and again and again with my eyes. I reached out and jiggled the knob, wanting to find the door unlocked. I turned and looked over my shoulder at the parking lot again for Edward's car, hoping my eyes had played a trick on me this time. The space where his car had been was still empty. You think I'd be happy, but the sense of guilt wouldn't let me be.

My apartment was dark, and I knew it was empty too. I unlocked the door and stepped inside. Making my way around like a cat in the blackness of night, I sat down on the sofa and for once in my life was very aware of what it felt like to be alone.

Sixty-One

There are some nights when you wish you'd wake up in the morning in a different place, or not wake up at all. This was one of them. As usual, I set the alarm clock for 5:32am. No matter how weird some might think those two minutes are, this part of my routine never changed either. I didn't awake at all during the night. The beeping of the alarm clock going off quickly reminded me that I had not been so fortunate as to become lost in a dream, destined for a hazy world beyond my own where we don't need or desire boyfriends.

I reset the clock for sixteen minutes ahead and stepped into the shower, taking full advantage of the time I allotted myself for a hot shower. I was just toweling off when the alarm sounded at 5:48am. Today was Monday, the beginning of the second week of the month. It was a cereal and cold milk day. I'll have this for breakfast three times this week and hot oatmeal with a banana on the other two days. It definitely felt like a cold milk day. I watched television and ate my cereal, eyeing the clock for it to be 6:32am when I'd leave for work.

I sat the bowl in the sink and had my hand on the door knob at 6:31am, standing there as if the red digital change from one to two was a gun in the air signaling the start of a marathon. I stood there so quiet and still and focused; I could practically here the electronic switch of numbers. Without looking, I reached up and traced the 32 on the door with one hand while locking the apartment with the other. Down 32 steps to Roosevelt Avenue and pacing my steps five blocks to work, I made it to The Latte Da right on time as usual.

Sallie was inside busying herself with the pastry case like every morning. When the bell on the door rang, she looked up and greeted me with a tight smile but with tears streaming down her face. Although I wasn't expecting this, I somehow knew what was wrong.

It had been months since I'd ever seen her look like this, since before she even met Charlie. Her tears for Auden in the hospital did not even look like this. Long ago in a drunken stupor on our nights out, she'd sometimes break down in tears and blubber about how much she was sad for being so alone and not having anyone. I knew she wasn't drunk now, but the sadness in her face looked emotively familiar.

"Is today the first day of the rest of our lives?" I asked.

Her eyes blinked to hold back another tear and she nodded at me in careful agreeance. Wiping her face, she busted into a sloppy mess of laughing and crying. I hugged her, admiring the smell of scones in her flour powdered hair.

"He said I was too simple and he was falling out of love with me," Sallie said into my shirt.

"You are far from simple," I told her.

"What about you?" she asked.

"In not so many words, I'm a cheater."

"I don't believe that."

Since Edward had actually left without calling me anything, I didn't reply.

"I'm boring," I added instead.

"Maybe we are too boring and simple to them. They will be boring and simple to someone else. Someone else will want us just the way we are."

I wished she was right. I don't want to change for anyone. I certainly didn't want either of us to be alone the rest of our lives, but for now—for this time in between—we had each other.

"Let's go out tonight. Just you and me, like old times," Sallie said.

That was definitely the medicine we both needed. The concoction of college beer, loud music, and fried foods will help anyone to forget their sorrows.

Like old times, it was just me and Sallie out that night. Too many margaritas and too much laughter convinced us to go back to her apartment. We took the milk from her fridge and poured it into a pitcher. We washed out the jug and took it with us to a little convenience store where we filled the jug up with a gallon of gas. We parked on the street several homes down from

200

Charlie's. Walking quietly up the sidewalk with the jug of gas tucked between us, we never once worried about getting caught. It was late and the street was dark. When we reached Charlie's lawn, we sloppily spelled out the word LOSER by pouring the gas on his yard. Although the temptation to strike a match was strong, we decided not to. The grass would die overnight and our message would be there for him in the morning, and for everyone who walked by.

Revenge. If that's what this was, it made Sallie feel better. I didn't feel like Edward would seek out reciprocation on me, but if he did, I was at least glad I didn't have a front yard.

Sixty-Two

When straight boys aren't getting laid, apologies ensue. They aren't verbal apologies though. Charlie had sent flowers to The Latte Da almost every day since he broke up with Sallie. She refused to call him. Neither Auden nor I proceeded to coax her into picking up the phone. On the first day, she threw the roses in the trash can. She refused the second delivery that came later that day.

"Do you want them?" she asked the next day when daisies came.

"I think I'm allergic."

She gave them to a customer, but more arrangements followed. She tossed the card and tried to tell Auden they were for him. He didn't believe her. When the front counter and her office were crowded with vases, Sallie decided to hold a drawing. For a dollar a ticket, we raffled off eight arrangements in one day and raised sixty dollars. Sallie put the money in our tip jar for us to split. By the end of that week, no more flowers came.

"I think he's given up," Auden said.

"Notice he hasn't called once. He hasn't even stopped by," Sallie said.

"I guess he is expecting you to call," I said.

"Why should I? *He* broke up with me. Would you call him?" she yelled.

"Probably not," I said.

"I don't even like flowers. They are fine for a birthday or Valentine's, and expected, but this shit is ridiculous. Be a man and pick up the phone," she spit into the air.

"Would you take him back?" Auden asked.

Silence.

"No. No, I don't think I would," she finally answered.

I believed her. If Charlie had not bombarded her with flowers, if he had just picked up the phone and called her or even come down to the shop and delivered flowers in person, I think he would have been given a second chance. Little did he know, the flowers only made her angrier. It was the wrong approach to winning her back, and in her eyes it was proof that Charlie didn't really know her well at all. By now, she'd stayed awake at night cursing his name. She'd shook her head in disgust each time a bouquet of flowers came through the door. Charlie had let too much time pass.

Charlie never did call or come by, and it was probably better that he didn't. If he showed up now, she'd probably hit him. If there were any vases of flowers left, she'd probably hurl one at him.

Sixty-Three

"Are you going tonight?" Auden asked me at work on Friday in between shifts.

"Going where?"

"They are announcing the photography contest winners tonight at the school. There will be free food, drinks, and live music."

"Wow! With everything that's been going on, I'd completely forgotten about the contest. It seems like that was forever ago."

"Are you going to go?"

"Well, since I'd forgotten about it—"

"Let's go together. Want to?"

"Okay. That sounds fun."

Relations between me and Auden had healed over time, like everything else. He wasn't second in line to Edward. He wasn't my back-up. Unsuspected events in our days have a strange way of changing our heart I guess and putting us onto a different course. I don't think Auden secretly liked me anymore, if he ever did.

After all, I was the plain, unfashionable, boring, photo-taking, number crazed, unfaithful, obsessive compulsive coffee barista with no opinion. Auden was a fairytale tattoo laced, pale, greased, freakish, Goth artist. We were two totally different works of art hanging on opposite walls in a museum. We were unique together, but probably not meant to go together.

Jake and his friend covered the closing shift for Auden that night so he could go. I went home after work to get ready and came back to meet Auden at the end of his shift. Tonight's event still didn't start for an hour. To kill time, we walked to the school instead of taking a bus.

"So what do you think my chances are of winning?"

"I heard there were over five hundred entries," Auden said, "Are you going to be disappointed if you don't?"

"Not really."

"What if you win?"

"I'll take you and Sallie out to dinner."

"You should spend the prize money on yourself."

"I didn't say dinner would be an expensive one."

He laughed. This small talk between us was nice, but I somehow sensed that Auden was really itching to ask me what happened between me and Edward. It was yet to be discussed between all of us at The Latte Da, and I was not going to offer up any information on my own. Not just yet. That's what I liked about Auden and Sallie. They respected me enough not to ask themselves. They knew whenever I'd want to talk about it, I'd come to them no matter how much they were dying on the inside to know.

Sallie had pretty much poured her heart out about Charlie that night after work. She was a mess all day at the shop and had to go to the back several times and shut the office door to cry. By the end of the night, her sadness had turned to anger. The trip to Charlie's house with the jug of gasoline had helped to cure that. By the end of the week, she was fine and there was nothing else to say. I knew she was still hurting on the inside, but on the outside she had moved on. She told me in the stock room that she wanted me to take her to a lesbian bar soon. She was giving up on men for a while.

"Have you ever dated women?" Auden asked me now.

"Never." I looked at him bright eyed, wondering where that question came from.

"Me neither."

"Have you ever dated anyone?" I had to ask.

"Not really. Not for any length of time anyway."

Unknowingly, Auden had opened the window to what I had wanted to know so long ago about him. I didn't have to hear it from Sallie. At last, I'd get the truth right from Auden himself. The mystery of his sexuality would be solved for me at last tonight.

"Is that something you want?"

"Sure. There's the dream of having someone in my life. But it's more like a fairy tale, I guess."

"Not one you have a tattoo of, I suppose."

"No."

"I'm no good at dating," I said outright.

"Why do you say that?" Auden asked with curiosity. I knew he was trying hard not to sound like he was fishing for gossip about what happened to Edward.

"It's the one thing I always fail at."

"We all do, Blaine. No one gets it right the first time."

"What about the second time, the third time, the fourth time, or the fiftieth time?"

"Ah, who's counting? To me, dating is like a blank canvas. I can paint whatever picture I want. It's not going to be perfect the first time. It might be bright and cheerful. It might be dark and dreary. If I don't like it, I can paint over it. And even start over."

"Or throw away that canvas and get a new one," I said sharply.

"Absolutely," Auden said. Not the answer I was expecting.

At the college, the photo contest gala was being held in a large stark white space. Auden told me it was commonly used for art shows and presentations, so the walls were often painted or props were brought it to fit the mood of what was on display. There was always art on display here open to the public, so it was sort of like a museum.

Now, it was set up to look like a professional photography studio. There were those black umbrellas with silver inner linings, used to focus light, on stands in each corner. There were three glass cases in the middle of the room. One held an old vintage camera from years ago. The middle one held an old 1980's Polaroid camera. The last case held a pocket size digital camera. They obviously represented how camera technology had progressed through the years.

On two walls opposite each other, all of the entries were hanging in a perfectly spaced checkerboard pattern completely covering the wall from the ceiling to the floor. Tables filled with food and beverages lined the other two walls. Crowds of people lined the walls of photos pointing out their pictures to their friends and family. A live band played boring ballads in the corner.

I'm not much for crowds outside of the bar, so Auden and I mingled toward the alcohol. The winners would not be announced for another hour, and the room continued to fill up with people. We were almost elbow to elbow like a crowded high school gymnasium on prom night. I felt a sweat break out on my forehead. Having not strayed too far from Auden, I approached him.

"Do you want to get out of here?" I asked.

"We haven't even looked for your photos."

"I don't care anymore," I lied. I did care, but not enough to stay in this growing sauna for another hour to see if I won. I had other things on my mind.

Auden looked puzzled. I focused my eyes on him letting him know I was serious as best I could.

"Are you okay? You look pale."

"It's all these people," I said. My nerves were unraveling. I felt like an anxious kid with their legs held together, begging their mother to find a restroom

"We could step outside for some air if you want?"

"I just want to go, Auden."

"Okay, we'll go."

We headed toward the door. Another gothic looking mime-like character stopped us near the exit to say hello to Auden. I could tell Auden didn't care to talk to him. He chattered on, not really giving Auden a chance to say anything. Auden didn't introduce me. Instead, Auden nodded with a blank expression as if he was more concerned with running away from this guy. I couldn't hear their conversation for all the people around us, but he awkwardly gave Auden a hug and then waved good-bye. Auden didn't hug him back.

When we reached the exit, I immediately felt better and my sense of claustrophobia had gone. We began walking through the campus towards the main highway. Neither of us had agreed upon anything, but I guess we were walking toward the bus stop.

"Who was that?" I asked when we had reached the exit and the crowd had cleared.

"Just a guy from a class I'm taking. He likes me." Auden didn't seem amused.

"Do you like him?" I asked.

"No. Couldn't you tell?"

"Why not?"

"He's annoying, and he's definitely not my type."

"You two looked like you had a lot in common."

"Just because both of us dress like this and wear eye shadow, Blaine, doesn't mean we have anything in common."

"What is your type then?" I asked him, instead of an apology.

"Short, plain clothed, shy, photogenic, obsessed with numbers, someone who likes walks in the park..."

"Sounds like someone I know."

"You of all people know him very well."

I didn't know what to say.

"Blaine, I want *you* to be my blank canvas."

"I'm no painting."

"What are you then?" he stopped walking and turned to ask me.

I thought for a moment.

"I'm more like a piece of clay. It took smooth trained hands and lots of time to mold me into this but I still have my flaws. I'm unique. One of a kind. Easily broken..." I said.

Auden replied, "I'm taking pottery class next semester."

Sixty-Four

We took a bus to Auden's apartment. It was near the interstate, on the edge of Midtown where groves of trees and concrete sound barriers block you from the busy traffic and the downtown lights just across the overpass. Auden's place was a spacious studio apartment with fourteen foot ceilings. Half walls divided the space into three sections. Canvases of all sizes and every color hung on every wall. It was reminiscent of the place we'd just left at the school, but not as crowded and much more amiable.

This was the first time I'd really seen any of Auden's work. He was a magnificent painter. Most were abstracts. There were several landscape paintings of fields and lakes and skies, but not your typical colors. The grass was painted in shades of purple and brown; the sky was yellow and orange.

He was also very talented with portraits. I couldn't believe the fine detail in some of the paintings he'd done of people I didn't know, but after looking at his work I felt like I knew a part of him. I flipped through the dozens of paintings stacked against the wall like books, surrounded by splatters of dried paint and jars of brushes. Because of my photography, I knew what it was like to come home to this. I knew what it was to come home everyday to something you love, something no one else really got about you.

Auden remained quiet while I admired his museum. From the corner of my eye, I noticed he was busying himself by collecting brushes and paints. He took a large blank canvas out of a closet and sat it up on an easel and pulled up a stool as if he was about to starting painting something. He sat down on the stool and watched me contently as I wandered around the room like a child choosing candy.

"Would you like to pose?" he asked coyly.

"For a painting?"

"Yeah."

"I'm no model."

I blushed and kept my eyes on the wall, avoiding eye contact with him.

"You don't have to be. Models are boring and fake anyway. I paint real people."

"Isn't it getting late?"

"It's only eight. They are just now announcing the winners back at the school. Are you upset now that we left?"

"No. Not at all. I haven't given it any thought since we walked away. Don't you have to work tomorrow?" I asked.

"So. You don't. Besides, I'm a night owl. I like staying up and having the night to myself. It's when I do my best work."

I was at a loss for words again, and a bit reticent about all of this.

"Pose for me," Auden pleaded.

"Where?"

"Grab that stool against the wall and pull it close."

He walked over and positioned me a few feet from him. He pulled up a floor lamp and turned it on. It had a soft gentle yellow light.

"Is that too bright?" he asked.

"Not at all. What should I do with my hands?"

"Just put them in your lap for now and relax your shoulders. Take a deep breath."

I did what he said, exhaling long and slow, arching my back to stretch my shoulders and release. I was biting my lip nervously.

"Relax. Don't bite your lip," Auden said with a laugh, tapping my chin with a finger.

He returned to his easel. Before sitting down, he pulled his shirt up over his head and tossed it onto the floor. I had seen his inked sleeves and back before. His chest was completely bare, except for a Celtic-like sun that circled his navel. The tattooed sleeves on his arms ended in a nice even round pattern at the collar bone and disappeared into his armpit. It made his front look sort of like he was wearing a vest. Auden was a walking piece of art himself.

"I like to paint in the nude. Clothes can be so restricting.

Makes me feel a bit freer. Is that okay?"

"Uh, sure. Okay. Fine by me."

"If it would make you uncomfortable—"

"No, it's fine. I promise. I know all about the need for expression. Do whatever it is you do to get you to that place."

"That place?" he asked.

He was casually playing with his nipple, his other hand resting on the rim of his khakis just above the zipper. I couldn't help but watch fixedly. I was becoming aroused.

"That mental state. That mode of creativity, you know? Whatever gets the creative juices flowing," I said. My eyes were scanning the walls again trying not to gawk at Auden.

"What gets your juices flowing, Blaine?"

We both busted into laughter at his question. Then, silence. Auden reached down and took off his boots in one swift movement, not even having to untie them. He threw them across the floor with a clump. He peeled off his white tube socks and tossed them across the room to join his boots. Unsnapping his pants and pulling down the zipper, he let his pants fall to his feet. He stepped out of them and pushed them aside with his foot. Thumbing the elastic of his black briefs, he hesitated for a moment while looking at me.

He had almost convinced himself, and I couldn't believe he'd gone this far. I think his inner debate over taking off his briefs was dependent upon how his penis was already reacting. A bulge was growing. I covered my eyes with a closed hand, opening my fingers to peek through. It made him laugh.

"Would it help if I were nude too?" I asked.

"You don't have to do that."

"I want to."

"Really?"

"Sure. Why not? Ever painted a nude?"

"Never actually. Not even at school. Do you want me to leave the room while you undress?" he asked.

"Where would you go?" I asked looking around.

"I could turn my back."

He spun around.

"That won't be necessary."

I stood up from the stool and began to slowly unbutton my shirt. Auden stood there next to his easel and patiently watched. I liked the feeling of his eyes on me as if I was performing a strip tease for him. I let my shirt fall off my shoulders and down to the floor. Pulling off each shoe and sock, I pushed them out of my way. I undid my pants and pulled them down along with my briefs. Pulling each pants leg off my feet, I tossed them over to my heap of clothes and then stood up completely nude there in front of Auden. His eyes fell below my waist just for a second and then quickly came back up to my eyes. He smiled with content.

"Your turn," I reminded him.

He slid his own briefs down his legs and gave a kick, sending them over to join the clothes pile. He shrugged as if saying, "Here I am." Here we were. I winked at him and then sat back down on the stool. He sat down behind his easel and chose a few tubes of paint from a drawer beneath the canvas. He squirted some paint from each tube onto a white plastic inlay, serving as a pallet, which pulled out of the easel like another drawer. Quiet at first, he began to coat the canvas with one or two colors using quick strokes with a wide brush. He dabbed it into a jar of water in between several strokes. I admired the wet clouds of pail color that developed in the water. I wanted to take a picture.

I liked the whishing sound of his brush against the canvas. It was very soothing. With my legs spread slightly apart, I rested my hands on top of each other between my thighs to shield my semi-erection from Auden's sight. From behind his easel I couldn't see much of him besides his feet and legs dangling beneath, and his head and right shoulder when he leaned to the side to look at me. It was the first time I think I'd ever been in a room with someone naked, but not touching them. It was quite a euphoric feeling.

Several calm hours passed. I was afraid to talk much for fear of Auden shushing me not to move. I spoke only when spoken to, and then it was out of the cracks of my mouth purposely trying not to budge. Auden's broad wild strokes made me wonder if his painting of me was going to be abstract.

"Do you paint all of your boyfriends?" I finally asked.

"Are you my boyfriend now?" Auden asked.

"You know what I mean."

"I've actually never had a boyfriend," Auden said.

"I don't believe that."

"I'm serious. I don't know why we're supposed to be looking for another being to complete us. Certainly there are people that make life more interesting. Isn't that what life is – a culmination of people and experiences? I just want to live life to its fullest right now. There was a time I felt as though I was living my life for everyone except myself. Not anymore."

"You've never wanted to spend the rest of your life with just one person?" I asked.

"Is that what a boyfriend is?"

"I guess so."

I really wasn't for sure anymore. Auden always had a way of speaking that caused me to look at things from a whole new perspective I'd never considered before. Maybe that was why I enjoyed the pleasure of his company. Maybe that was why I was sitting across from him now completely nude, but not too concerned about it.

"I prefer the word lover. It can apply to both someone long term or short term. We all like the idea of spending the rest of our lives with one person, but that idea is further out of reach than we anticipate, don't you think?"

"It's a goal to strive toward, I guess."

"Did you ever once think you'd spend the rest of your life with Edward?"

"Sure. I thought about it."

"That's the giddy feeling of love telling your brain that. Love is so immature," he said with harder strokes on the canvas now accentuating each word almost as if he was taking anger out on the canvas.

"I loved Edward; at least I thought I did."

"And look at you now."

"Point taken."

"Don't worry. I'm not trying to offend you. What happened to Edward anyway? Mind me asking?"

I had not even told Sallie yet what happened between me and Edward. It's hard to admit to someone the mistakes you made, at least until you are ready to confess. Remember what I told you, no one likes to be reminded of their mistakes. That's why we deny them. Sitting here naked across from my tattooed coworker changed that. I don't think there was anything I could have said that would shock him or make him think badly of me. I had revealed myself physically to him, unscathed, sitting here beneath the yellow light; somehow opening up emotionally to him seemed only natural.

Auden put down his brush to give me his full attention. He said the canvas needed to dry a bit anyway. He wouldn't let me take a break to look at it. He said I couldn't see it anyway until it was finished. I told him about the day I was busy preparing my entries for the contest. I tried to remain fair to Edward, but admitted that he was just in the way that day. I might have been wrong for ignoring Edward's ideas of me becoming a professional photographer, or maybe I should have just been more open minded. In just telling myself this out loud, I realized I didn't care about his opinion because inside I knew that it was not going to work between Edward and me. We were polar opposites and although some say opposites attract, I was ignoring the fact that my time with Edward would be coming to an end sooner or later.

We ignore our long term unhappiness possibly because of the short term happiness that someone does give us. I loved going to bed with Edward every night. I enjoyed our love making. I coveted waking up next to him every morning. Outside of that, the countless hours spent with him through the day bored me. We never had much to say to each other outside of talking about work. Several weeks of small talk over teaching and coffee making gets stale.

Without even knowing what we were doing or why, we sought out things to do together that didn't require talking. We watched television and hung out with Charlie and Sallie, or we went to movies. We did all the things that Edward wanted to do. When we were forced into everyday scenarios where conversation was eminent, neither of us liked what the other had to say. Both of us were boring individuals before we even met, with no way to cure each other's dullness.

"I don't think you are boring," Auden said, "I just don't think you like yourself. If you don't like yourself, Blaine, how can you expect anyone else to?"

Auden was right. I needed someone to tell me the truth, just like Randy had that night in the bar. Edward deserved to hear the truth too. No matter how cliché it sounded, the truth had set us free. I had to stop beating myself up over cheating on Edward after one small argument. If it had not come to this, I might still be beating myself up over just being with him. Neither of us deserved such agony.

"That's why I don't have boyfriends," Auden said. "I don't need companionship just to be happy."

"So you don't think I'm a bad person for cheating on him?" I asked, raising my eyebrow. I was afraid of his reaction but knew he'd be honest.

"That doesn't make you a bad person. If anything, it proves you're a man. We all have desires. Monogamy can be quite a struggle, especially among gay men for some reason. Why do you think men cheat on their house wives after thirty years of marriage?"

"Boredom, I guess."

"Like I said, it's definitely a struggle. But you and Edward weren't together very long, so I wouldn't worry about it. See, it was the way out, what you wanted all along, and you didn't even know it."

"If I had, I would have cheated on him a long time ago."

What a horrible thing to say, right? But it's not fair to be with anyone if one of you isn't happy. You cheat each other out of the real happiness you'd be having without them. Sort of like my jar of wishes I had tucked away in the closet.

Wishes that weren't mine.

Sixty-Five

We must have talked for at least an hour. I had lost all track of time ever since we got started, and I didn't care. I looked over to the window, focusing on the reflection of Auden and the canvas against a black night blanketed with stars. The shine of the yellow light above me made it impossible to focus on the detail of the painting.

I thought of a movie I saw where an old eccentric movie maker got his handsome young gardener to pose for drawings. He coaxed the young man into posing shirtless so he could admire his physique. Although the old man was eager just to reach out and touch another human, he more or less desired the boy for daily conversation. When the young man accuses the old man of sexual intentions, he rips the sketch pad from the man's hand only to discover chicken scratch drawings of lines and circles. It was all for companionship and to pass the time. The old man had not drawn a thing.

I trusted Auden enough, even before tonight, to know this was not an elaborate set up for us two to sit down and have a heart-to-heart. His painting, of me or not, would be faultless and probably something that would take my breath away. I couldn't wait to see it, but it was the farthest thing from my mind now. I didn't want my time tonight with Auden to ever end.

"What time is it?" I asked.

"Just past midnight," Auden said, leaning over to look at a clock on a shelf behind me. "Do you need to go?"

"No, I'm okay if you are."

"Sure. Stay awhile. So what was your picture of for the contest again?"

"Truthfully?"

"Is there any reason to lie about them now?"

"You got me there. My main entry was of you."

"Me?" Auden asked with surprise, putting down his brush again and looking at me.

"Yep."

216

"When did you take a photo of me?"

"In the park downtown that day. Remember?"

"In Bachardy Park? You weren't there. There was only an old man and his cat."

"You sat down on the bench next to the old man. His cat was on a leash. He handed you a piece of bread to feed to the pigeons."

"Where were you?"

"Lying on the ground in the bushes."

"Were you hiding from me?"

"Not exactly. I was already lying down with my camera. I was a bit shocked to see you there, so I didn't reveal myself. Sorry."

"That's okay. So what was the picture of?"

"You and the old man and the cat sitting on the bench. I snapped a picture just as he was handing you the bread. I hope you aren't mad at me."

"No. I can't wait to see the picture," he said, picking up a brush again and turning back to the painting.

"Auden? Why'd you come to the park that day?"

He was quiet for a beat, carefully selecting his words in his head.

"I wanted to talk to you," he said not looking back at me.

"About what?" I had a feeling I already knew what he'd say but I asked anyway.

"Honestly, I don't even know now what I would have said to you. I wanted to apologize for being short with you. I've always had a bit of a crush on you, Blaine, but it was like you were blind to noticing. Then, Edward came into the picture, and I got jealous. It was my fault for not speaking up earlier, and for thinking you'd be interested once I got up enough nerve to tell you how I felt."

"*You* were actually interested in me? Honestly, Auden, I didn't even know you were gay until a few months ago. I had to ask Sallie. I'm sorry."

Sallie had already insinuated that Auden liked me a long time ago, but I had just met Edward. I think I liked the idea of suddenly being the center of attention, but I wasn't listening to my heart. My heart truly wanted to be with Auden. I think my brain liked the excitement of the blind date with Edward. I'd never been on a blind date before. Or maybe I felt I owed it to Sallie to go out with him since he was Charlie's best friend.

"Don't be sorry. I'm sorry that we've worked together this long at the coffee shop and only now have we really gotten to know each other better. Who knew that sitting down nude with each other would bring out all of this?" he said.

It didn't happen very often, if at all, that I'd ever sat down with anyone nude except for in the dark; and there definitely wasn't any talking. Now I know why they always tell you to picture your audience naked in order to relax when standing in front of them to give a speech.

"It's almost one in the morning. Would you like to just stay the night?" Auden asked.

"I can call a cab if you want me to go."

"I want you to stay."

Auden put his brushes in a jar of water and walked it over to the kitchen sink. He walked over to me and turned off the lamp. Taking me by the hand, he led me over to his platform bed tucked away in the corner behind one of the half walls. We laid down, silent and facing each other. Street lamps shining in through the windows slowly faded the darkness so we could just see each other.

I reached up to his face and traced one of his scars from the break-in with my finger. He pulled my hand away gently, not wanting to be reminded of what had happened. He held my hand to his mouth and kissed it gently. I leaned in closer to him, but he put his other hand to my chest.

"Let's just sleep tonight. Hold each other and sleep."

I nuzzled in to the pictures inked on his shoulder and closed my eyes with content. I wished this night would never end, but then I thought of what Auden had said about just living for the moment. So, if I had been standing at a fountain, I think I would have kept my wish to myself then.

Sixty-Six

We awoke just a few hours later to bright sunlight filling the room. I don't remember an alarm clock announcing the arrival of sun. I only stirred because Auden had to unwrap himself from my arms to get out of bed.

"Do you take the bus to work?"

"I usually walk, but if I do today I'll be late. I let us sleep in a little," he said.

"I'll wait and take the bus with you back to Midtown."

"I'd like that."

Auden showered and dressed. I collected my clothes from the floor and went into the bathroom when he was finished. I splashed some water on my face and attempted to part my hair. On the bus ride back to Midtown I felt like I was on a caravan returning from some holy place. I felt rejuvenated and had forgotten about the monotony and routine of my days. It was the first day of the rest of my life all over again, another X on the calendar to judge everything going forward by.

"I have something for you," Auden said as we stepped off the bus just a few blocks between the coffee shop and my apartment.

"What is it?" I asked with curiosity because he was not carrying anything with him, not even the leather bag I was accustomed to seeing him come into The Latte Da with.

From his back pocket, he pulled out several blue lined pages that were folded in half and in half again, a perfect square with frayed edges from where it had been ripped from a notebook. He handed them to me.

"Remember the day you told me you were going to go to the University to see what Edward looked like? Remember what I told you to do?"

"You said to take a notebook and write everything down."

"Did you?"

"Yeah, but I never had the chance to give it to Edward."

"Remember you asked me if I'd ever written down

anything about someone?"

"I do remember that. You said you didn't write. You paint."

"I lied. I did write something down." Auden acknowledged the pieces of paper with his eyes. I started to unfold it but he stopped me. "Not now. Read it at your apartment, when you are alone."

I said good-bye to Auden, and told him I might stop in later to have lunch with him if he'd like. I tucked the pieces of paper into my pocket. Instead of going to my apartment, I decided to walk back to the art school to see who won.

The campus was just as beautiful as Bachardy Park with its tall trees and neatly kept walkways. Foliage and wild flowers in large antique-looking planters lined the entries to all of the buildings. Odd metal sculpture sat in plazas or next to buildings, like strange satellites that had landed one day and just been left there. My favorite was a large metal beetle, sitting in the middle of a bed of daisies, and made from rusty old car parts.

Last night's crowd had long since cleared. Some servicemen were at the front of the auditorium clearing away the banquet tables. Only the photography umbrellas, now unlit were still in the room. One had even fallen out of its metal tripod and was lying on the ground like confetti or a party hat long after the party is over. The three glass cases that were in the middle of the room were still there but now empty and covered in smudged fingerprints. An empty wine glass sat on top of one them. Like the day after a wild party with the revelers all gone, the auditorium seemed torn and hollow. The spotlights in the ceiling that lit the walls of all the photographs were dim. I searched the wall for a switch to turn them back up. An electrical hum brought the sleeping walls back to life.

Like a tourist with a museum hall all to themselves, I took my time pacing back and forth along each wall to admire all the entries. There were three pictures now hanging on the main wall on a field of black. Probably the winners. I took my time approaching them, first giving all the others the attention they deserved. There were so many portraits, flowers, children blowing out candles, dogs chasing tennis balls, and butterflies on branches. I was amazed at how many people see beauty in the exact same things. What's wrong with the rest of the world we aren't looking at?

I eventually found my second and third entry among the roses, fruit bowls, and Christmas trees. I did not find the picture of Auden there among them. It was hanging on the main wall in the third place spot. I was runner up to a single daisy bloom, probably snapped at the Botanical Gardens, and a sunset over the downtown bridge. They were picture perfect postcards anyone in this city had seen before.

And then there was my picture of Auden, the old man, and the cat sitting on the park bench in a whirlwind of pigeons. It was definitely something no one else had seen before, or at least I thought it was. I mean everyone has seen flowers and sunsets. There was nothing about the first and second place photographs that stood out to me now making me think they earned to be there. But obviously, someone, some judge thought they were better than my picture. It just proved my point again that no one wants to face the truth. We'd rather cover it up with sunsets and roses.

The raw edge I thought I'd captured in the park that day was a kind reality that made you take notice. It made you think about what the old man was wondering while looking at Auden. Why did he have a cat on a leash? Would Auden take the bread from the old man? It made me think. These were the questions I thought would be conjured up when judging my photograph. If the two pictures that beat me had inspired questions of my own, I'd been happy with my third place win. But they didn't.

I turned around to see if the men were done clearing away the tables. They were. It was just me in a sea of shared memories, boring snapshots we framed on our wall or emailed to relatives for a pat on the back. I'd been guilty of a few myself. I walked back over to one of the gallery walls and chose a photo of a fat chubby birthday princess with a snaggled tooth fairy grin, smiling over a candle lit homemade cake. I took her down off the wall. I then took my picture of Auden down and replaced it with the birthday girl. With my photo tucked under my arm, I walked out of the auditorium and went home.

Sixty-Seven

I'm not a sore loser. After all, I did come in third out of all those entries, and I could definitely use the one hundred dollar prize money. Auden didn't seem to mind when I told him he was my subject matter in the photo. And he didn't even know I'd taken the photo anyway. But none of those reasons mattered to me now as I stole my photo away.

Something new and thrilling had developed between Auden and me last night. I didn't even know what it was, if anything, but I knew I wasn't ready to share it with anyone. Like when Sallie kept Charlie to herself, even when Edward and I coupled off for a while, I wanted Auden all to myself for now. This odd "lover" relationship, or whatever he may choose to call it, was mine for now. The photo had nothing to do with where we were now really, except it was a reminder to me that if I had revealed myself to Auden that day in the park, things might have been different.

No matter how much we have the opportunity to see where we went wrong, and no matter how much we wish we could go back and change it, we shouldn't regret that path we chose. I don't. The photo just proves to me that this is the right time for all of this to be happening. Each of our lives needed to set some other things in motion, molding us for when this day would finally come. Back when I took this photo, I had not even been sure if Auden was gay or not, much less if he liked me. And who is to say we would have ended up where we are now if I had crawled out of the bushes to speak to him that day in the park? It's still fun to imagine "what if."

If I could I'd go back to that Saturday with Edward when I was getting my entries ready for the contest, I think I'd left this one of Auden out. I'd kept it to myself, to eventually share with Auden only because he'd know what it really meant. I'd choose a different photo to submit, but it too would probably be lost on the wall with all the other photos just like my other two entries. The photos we take of the memories we share with each other are the only things that distinguish how we remember them. This memory was mine, and I wasn't ready to share it with anyone.

At home, I wrapped the photo in plain brown paper and tucked it into my bag to carry with me to lunch. I was going to give it to Auden as a gift. I traced the numbers on the door, counted the steps down, and walked the five blocks to The Latte Da in my usual 160 steps. Some things aren't meant to change.

Like twins who can read each other's thoughts, Auden and I just smiled at each other when I walked in the door. Sallie came up to me and hugged my neck when she saw me loitering in the lobby.

"What are you doing here today?" she asked.

"Auden and I are going to lunch together."

"Ohhhhh," she said, smiling at me and turning to look at Auden very threatening like. He busied himself with wiping down the espresso machine to avoid her. "We need to all go out sometime. I want you to go with me to this bar I heard about. It's called the Midtown Flame."

"Lesbians?" I asked.

"You've heard of it?"

"No. Just a lucky guess. Are you going to start wearing a tool belt and riding a Harley?"

"Is that what lesbians do?"

"Sallie, I have no idea what lesbians do. I'll go to the bar with you, but you are on your own with the rest."

"Auden, will you go? How about tonight?" she asked.

"Sure, I'll go. I love lesbians," he replied.

An old man sitting in the lobby looked up with curiosity at what Auden had just said. He shook his head in disbelief and went back to reading his paper. The three of us broke into laughter.

Sixty-Eight

Although there was sawdust on the floor, I also expected to find flannel wallpaper at the Midtown Flame. It was country line dancing night, so there was plenty of flannel on the patrons. The crowd was half women and half men, or quite possibly Auden and I were the only men in the joint. With all the sports bras, peach fuzz moustaches, and butch hair cuts some of the men were probably women. Too bad I left my camera at home.

Sallie glued herself to a table in the corner and made us make trips to the bar. She begged us to hurry because she did not want to be left alone for very long. Lesbians are much nicer than men at the bar. Several of them approached us first to chat and immediately asked if we were a couple. They politely asked to admire Auden's tattoos, and even showed us a few of their own. They also asked about the new girl in town sitting with us at our table.

"Would she dance with me if I asked her?" one handsome lady asked.

"I'll make her," Auden teased.

"Watch out! She'll tear that dance floor up," I threw in.

"What's her name?" she asked.

"Sallie," Auden and I said in unison.

"That's my mother's name. This must be fate."

And with that, we held back a little and watched as the dyke approached our innocent little Sallie, sitting there at the table all alone trying not to make eye contact with anyone. She said no at first, but the persistent woman took her by the hand and got down on one knee. Whatever she said made Sallie laugh and blush and she got up to accompany the women to the floor. Walking away, she looked over at us and winked. We tried to look dumbfounded.

"Is she going to dance with her purse?" Auden said when he noticed the strap on Sallie's shoulder and the bag at her hip.

"Maybe *that's* what lesbians do," I said.

"I thought they carried wallets on a chain."

In between the country tunes, the DJ played hip hop. It was an odd mix of sound that probably chased the gay men away, who were accustomed to acid-tripping techno and heavy bass.

"Oh, heck, why should Sallie have all the fun? Dance with me?" Auden asked.

"Sure."

We set our drinks down and Auden took my hand to lead me to the floor. As the gyrating crowd circled the floor, we eventually ended up next to Sallie and her partner. Before she had noticed us, the lights dimmed to a glowing red and a ballad came on. Auden and I looked around and watched the female couples wrap their arms around each other for a slow dance. Sallie did the same.

"I feel like I'm at prom," I said.

"Did you go to an all girl school?" Auden joked.

"No, but these are not girls. They're lesbians."

Auden put his arms around my waist to pull me close. I had never slow danced before, but I liked the idea of it now.

"This is definitely fate," he whispered in my ear.

A sudden bright light from over our shoulder caught our attention. We turned to see Sallie holding a disposable camera to her face. Her dance partner was standing there holding Sallie's purse. When we turned toward her, she snapped a photo again.

"Smile, guys," she called out.

Despite the white dots now dancing in front of my eyes from the bright flash, I did my best to smile. Auden kissed me on the cheek and Sallie snapped another photo, capturing this memory forever. It was a memory worth remembering for us all.

A few days later I took a bus down to Bachardy Park. I had not been there since the day I took the photo of Auden. Like an old friend, its tall trees and flocking pigeons welcomed me. The pigeons cooed their hellos and then turned their attention to a little kid and his mom buying popcorn from the street vendor. Déjà vu. An old man with brown paper bag skin sat on a park bench reading a black leather-bound book. I didn't have my camera with me today. I didn't need it.

I took a seat on an empty bench, facing the fountain, and

pulled from my pocket a photo Sallie had given me. It was from that night at the Midtown Flame. Her dance partner had taken the photo while Sallie posed with her arms around me and Auden. Our smiles were huge and toothy and our eyes were bloodshot. Mine were even demon red from the cheap exposure. It didn't matter though. I think this was the first photo anyone had taken of me since my senior yearbook picture. This was my close up, ready or not.

I would not obsess over the flaws. The ones in the photo were trite. The ones not shown here were just parts of life. There was a time when I'd feel the need to obsess over such things, for no real reason at all. Not anymore.

Sixty-Nine

Three or four months later, Auden gave his notice at The Latte Da. We'd discussed it over Chinese takeout the night before, so it wasn't a surprise to me like it was to Sallie. Auden landed a job teaching at an art school in Savannah, Georgia. He had already told me weeks ago about applying. He took time off from work to fly down for an interview.

I'd still never read those pieces of paper he gave to me with the words he jotted down the first time he'd ever seen me. When he was out of town, it felt like the right time to read them but I still waited. If he got the job and was going to leave, I didn't want to make it more painful for myself to say good-bye.

Auden never asked me to go with him. Remember, this new relationship between us was not to be serious. He wouldn't allow it. If anything, it'd taught me that we don't have to have someone we call a "boyfriend" in order to not seem so alone in life. Friendships last much longer, and although Auden and I had slept together, that was another lesson I'd learned. Sometimes when we are making those wishes, we forget to ask for how long we want our wish to last for.

Our friendship, outside of work, had different boundaries. Both of us allowed the other to date anyone else at anytime, but we never did. We didn't spend every night together; after all, we did work together and saw each other almost every day anyway. The lines between being coworkers and being "lovers" were never crossed. They just sort of merged.

There were no reasons to cross off the days on the calendar and mark anniversaries of time we spent together. I never had to worry that at any moment, this could end between us. If I did find someone else, or if Auden did, we would accept that. But I don't think either of us was looking. But Auden's true love was art, so I couldn't blame him when I found out he was looking to leave the city.

Sallie didn't go with me to the airport to see him off. She'd already said her good-byes. At the terminal before boarding his plane, Auden presented me with a wrapped canvas. It was the painting he'd done of me that night. I had forgotten about it because he never asked me to pose for the painting again. He finished it from memory.

The portrait was like looking into a mirror. Actually, it was of me looking into a mirror. The reflection in the mirror was bug-eyed and biting his nails. He wore a camera around his neck and was also wearing a shirt with the number 32 on it. The "me" looking into the mirror was just a plain and calm silhouette, intended to be the shadow of myself now looking at the painting.

"You are much different now than you used to be," Auden said.

"I have you to thank for that."

"Nah, you should thank yourself, Blaine. You're the one who's changed."

"I'm still a single obsessive compulsive coffee barista. Nothing has changed about that."

"We can't change who we are, Blaine, only how we look at ourselves."

I stayed until his plane had disappeared into the clouds.

Seventy

Auden's painting hangs in my apartment. I've still never read those first words he wrote. The pieces of paper he gave me are lost in a drawer somewhere. I still set my alarm clock at the same intervals every morning. I still go to the park and take pictures occasionally, and pour coffee for Sallie at The Latte Da. I still trace the brass numbers on my apartment door and count the steps leading downstairs. The only thing different is that it's not so much a routine anymore, as it is just a part of life.

Sallie and I still have couples night out. She still drinks too much and dates women. I occasionally work the bathroom at the Mexican bar or the dance floor at Backstreet. The only thing different is that we don't beat ourselves up over the mistakes we've made, the choices we make. We're content without steady men in our lives. It is just a part of life.

I'll turn 33 next month. I'm not going to move or try to bribe my land lord to change my apartment number. I'm not sure how I'll feel about the number 32 after that, only that I'll remember the year I was 32 years old as being a year of many lessons learned. I'm sure there will be much more to learn at 33, 34 and yes, even 35. That's life.

Now that you know this, you finally know all you need to. And the parts you don't are the details I've left out, the Kodak moments in your own album. We've shared those from day one, you and me. They are a piece of us we all know inside and out. Everyone does. No one has to share them out loud, or run to get a photo book off the shelf as proof. We know them by heart.

I decided to take that jar of coins down out of the closet. Like a kid eager to cash in his savings, I held the jar between my legs while taking the bus downtown. Walking through the park, I didn't look over each shoulder this time. I didn't care who saw me. Approaching the fountain in the middle, I unscrewed the lid to the jar. I raised it into the air over the basin and let the coins trickle out. Birds that had been dipping into the water up on the second tier flew away from the jingling sound of the coins falling. The water splashed my face as the weight of the jar lightened. When the jar was empty, I exhaled and sat down.

So today I sit here on a bench in Bachardy Park passively but cameraless, my shutter still open, recording.

Thinking, but not wishing for, not obsessing over anything at all right now.

ABOUT THE AUTHOR

Shannon Yarbrough is an author, painter, and poet originally from Tennessee. He has lived in St. Louis, Missouri since late 2001. His first novel, *The Other Side of What*, was published in 2003. Visit Shannon on the web at www.shannonyarbrough.com.

Printed in the United Kingdom by
Lightning Source UK Ltd., Milton Keynes
137355UK00001BA/2/P